WASTE OF A LIFE

WASTE OF A LIFE

Simon Brett

SEVERN
HOUSE

First world edition published in Great Britain and the USA in 2022
by Severn House, an imprint of Canongate Books Ltd,
14 High Street, Edinburgh EH1 1TE.

Trade paperback edition first published in Great Britain and the USA in 2023
by Severn House, an imprint of Canongate Books Ltd.

severnhouse.com

British Library Cataloguing-in-Publication Data
A CIP catalogue record for this title is available from the British Library.

ISBN-13: 978-0-7278-5069-0 (cased)
ISBN-13: 978-1-4483-0793-7 (trade paper)
ISBN-13: 978-1-4483-0792-0 (e-book)

All Severn House titles are printed on acid-free paper.

Typeset by Palimpsest Book Production Ltd.,
Falkirk, Stirlingshire, Scotland.
Printed and bound in Great Britain by
TJ Books, Padstow, Cornwall.

To
the Memory of my Brother
Michael

ONE

'd been seeing Cedric regularly for some months before the day I found him dead.

I should explain the basics. My name is Ellen Curtis. My company's called SpaceWoman and, though the word 'company' might suggest a copious array of staff, it is in fact just me.

What I do is decluttering. Because so many people get it wrong, I should emphasize that I don't do house clearance. My services are called on when the amount of clutter people have accumulated gets out of hand. I then advise them on what to throw away, what to find a new home for, and how to manage what remains in a way that prevents the whole cycle from starting up again.

Though SpaceWoman deals primarily with the physical practicality of moving stuff around, I often find that the building-up of clutter has a mental dimension too. Just as one is recommended to have a healthy mind in a healthy body, so a disordered home can reflect a disordered mind. And fragments of minds don't pack away into boxes and binbags as conveniently as visible rubbish.

I should also say at this point that my services don't come accompanied by moral lessons. None of that 'cleanliness is next to godliness' stuff with me. Nor do I get excited about the concept of objects 'sparking joy'. I don't tell people how to live their lives. Beyond considerations of personal safety, I'm not there to advise my clients what they should do. My approach relies on suggestion rather than prescription.

And I frequently find that my relationship with a client continues long after the initial job has been done. There are a good few I continue to keep an eye on months – or even years – after I've delivered what I was contracted for. Some of them need the ongoing support and some of them have become friends.

Cedric was a case in point. Like many of my clients, he was

referred to me by the local social services in Chichester, which is where I live. He's there too, in a terraced house, 14 Seacrest Avenue, a quiet suburban road on the other side of the railway line from the city centre, in other words far from the cathedral, the market cross, Chichester Festival Theatre and the tourist bits.

The reason Cedric Waites came to the attention of the authorities was that his son Roy, who lived in Worcester, and whose contact was restricted to a monthly phone call, got no reply one day when he called. He phoned one of Cedric's neighbours, Vi, who kept the vaguest of eyes on the old man. She went round to the house, where her knocking produced the same lack of response.

The police were alerted and, since no one had a key, they entered by force. Inside the hall, they found, amongst other debris, piles of dusty mail stacked up, suggesting that the front door had not been opened for some years.

Steeling themselves for an unpleasant discovery, they began to search the premises. Though no one local had much information about Cedric Waites, he was known to be in his late seventies, so the policemen's expectation was to find a body at some stage of decomposition.

But when they got up to the old man's bedroom, what they encountered was someone still alive. Not in a very good state, but alive. Clearly, Cedric had 'had a fall' – that ominous statement which is the precursor of so many worse afflictions among the elderly. He appeared to have slipped getting in or out of bed and got jammed between the frame and the wall. He hadn't had the strength to pull himself up and his phone was inaccessible the other side of the room.

Fortunately, it was a warm late spring, so during his entrapment, he hadn't died of hypothermia. Equally fortunately, the police had found him before he died of starvation.

He had been taken to Chichester's main hospital, St Richard's, where he was cleaned up. After treatment for various bruises and abrasions caused by the fall and his attempts to extricate himself, he was pronounced fit to go home.

Except, of course, his home wasn't fit to receive him. The police's break-in to a place which had been locked up for so long revealed a catalogue of health hazards. It would not be safe for Cedric Waites to take up residence again until certain safety measures had been put in place.

His recluse's unwillingness to allow anyone inside his house meant that various basic amenities were not functioning. The central heating boiler had not worked for some years. During the winters, Cedric's only form of heating appeared to have been an old-fashioned two-bar electric fire. An equally ancient Ascot heater over the kitchen sink was his only source of hot water.

Other domestic appliances had reached the end of their useful lives. The venerable Hoover had long since given up the ghost though, seeing the state of the place, using it had never been high on the old man's priorities. His television had broken down, too, so had the internet router. The presence of the latter suggested Cedric might once have had a working laptop, but I saw no evidence of one.

The landline had not worked for years, and his means of communication were reduced to a very archaic – and far from smart – mobile phone.

Basically, anything whose repair or replacement would have involved an engineer coming inside Cedric Waites's house had been allowed to expire naturally.

One item of kitchen equipment that did still work was the freezer, though it was in desperate need of defrosting. Its survival was important, because Cedric stored all of his food in there and, without it, he would have starved. There was also a much-discoloured microwave which appeared still to be in working order.

This state of affairs was discovered by the officers of the social services who had inspected the place while he was still in St Richard's. Had he been in residence, it is very unlikely that he would have allowed them in. An Englishman's home remains his castle, whatever state it's in. And, without complaints from neighbours or evidence of criminality taking place on the premises, it's up to the owner who he allows to come in.

It was at this point that the social services got in touch with me. I met for a briefing in their offices and pretty soon realized that Cedric Waites was going to be one of my more difficult clients.

*　　*　　*

Cedric wasn't difficult in himself. When I got through to him, I discovered a man of considerable charm and intelligence. It was the getting through that was difficult.

The way our first meeting was organized was familiar to me. It had happened with other hospitalized clients. The social workers who were to bring Cedric back from St Richard's arranged that I should be in his house when they arrived. That was likely to be late morning on the Monday, after he'd been passed fit by the doctor. They would not leave him alone at the house until he had had a discussion with me about the way forward. If that conversation didn't take place, or if he proved uncooperative, the implication was that he would be returned to St Richard's. Though, given the urgent demand for hospital beds, I'm not sure how realistic that threat was.

I had worked with the social services many times and knew exactly what they were doing. They wanted to get the client off their hands as soon as possible, and delegating his care to me was a good way of achieving that outcome. That's not a criticism. Funding cuts and the lack of foreign recruits after Brexit meant that there were far too few social workers. And those who survived were hopelessly overworked. From their point of view, any responsibility that could be subcontracted to someone else – like me – was good news.

I had been given the details of the hazards the police had found at 14 Seacrest Avenue and a copy of a key to the back door, which opened into the kitchen. It was the only entrance that Cedric apparently used, and I got there an hour before his scheduled return to assess the scale of the problem.

It was monumental. Not really an issue of hoarding. I've seen the inside of a lot of hoarders' houses, clambered on many occasions over ceiling-high piles of stuff to gain access to rooms, so I know what I'm talking about. And, except for in the kitchen and hall, there was quite a lot of space in Cedric's house. His reclusiveness meant he wasn't prone to going out on shopping sprees for stuff he didn't need, like so many hoarders. And the fear of answering the door to delivery men had prevented him from becoming an Amazon junkie.

One surprising find was a large amount of money. Secreted – no, that's the wrong word, there was no secrecy involved – *placed* under Cedric's bed. Blocks of twenty-pound notes, at least two thousand pounds, in rows in a black briefcase, like an assassin's payoff in some heist movie. About half the contents missing. But my suspicions were not moving towards criminality. Paying for everything by cash would appeal to a hoarder's mentality. The dust inside the briefcase suggested the withdrawal from the bank had taken place some years before.

And, as to the security aspect, if you're in your house all the time and never let anyone else inside, leaving a briefcase full of twenties under your bed is not really that much of a risk.

I hadn't noticed on my way up but, as I went back down, I was aware of a slight wobble on the staircase. Inspecting the steps, I felt damp on the carpet. Worse than damp, a kind of green slime. Tracing it back, the source was a leak from the upstairs lavatory. Clearly, water had been seeping out for some time, quite possibly years. One or two of the steps under the wet carpet felt soggy and soft. It was only a matter of time before they would rot through. The staircase was a potential deathtrap for an elderly man.

Back downstairs, I shuffled through the piles of discoloured envelopes shored up against the front door (now secured on the outside by a police padlock). A lot of them appeared to be brown-enveloped bills for domestic services. Perhaps the demise of the central heating was due, not to breakdown, but simply non-payment of the gas bill. Thank God, Cedric appeared to have kept his electricity connected. Maybe that was paid by direct debit.

The other debris that rendered the hall and kitchen virtually impassable suggested Cedric had had some means of getting nourishment into the house. All the rubbish was made up of rinsed-out food containers. Putting the bins out must have been something the old man had given up long ago. He didn't like stepping outside the house even for that.

The containers were stacked in what might once have been neat piles but had, over time, tumbled down into uneven pyramids with spreading foothills of debris. The level of dust on the bottom ones suggested they had been there for years. Most were for shop-bought microwavable meals, but some unbranded plastic boxes with handwritten stickers looked as if they had contained home-cooked dishes. So, Cedric must have set up some kind of local network arrangement to deliver food. From accommodating neighbours perhaps?

He did not hide his suspicion of me when the social workers brought him back to the house. Nor the resentment of the fact that I was already there, that I had been rootling around into his privacy.

But Cedric Waites was subdued, on his best behaviour. He was a realist. He understood the deal. If he agreed to take the steps suggested, the social workers would leave. Then he would only have my attentions to evade.

He looked at me with a level of calculation. Although he had only had hot water from the Ascot heater for some years, his clothes were clean and the social workers had not seen the necessity of getting him new ones. Doing what I do, you get inured to the smell of people who have given up on personal hygiene as much as they have on other aspects of their life, but Cedric Waites did not belong in that category. There was a kind of old-fashioned neatness about him and he spoke with the quiet dignity of an educated man. He also wore a tie, which marked him out as being of a certain generation.

I spelled out to him the necessity of getting the hot water and central heating working again. He denied that his gas supply had been cut off for non-payment.

Which made sense because my cursory examination suggested that he would need a new boiler. He meekly agreed that I could organize a heating engineer to come in and assess the situation. (Over the years doing SpaceWoman, I have built up a network of reliable tradespeople for this kind of work. Not only are they all expert at their jobs, they're also sensitive to the – sometimes unusual – needs of the clients in whose houses they'll be working. Most of them seemed to be called Dan, Don, or some similar variation. The heating engineer I had in mind was called Dean.)

Cedric didn't argue when I suggested I should contact BT to get his landline working again. And he seemed positively keen when I proposed getting the broadband router reconnected.

I also drew attention to the state of the staircase. Initially, that was going to require a plumber to sort out the leaking lavatory.

Then, if the steps were as rotten as they appeared to be, a carpenter would be needed too. Because it was a safety issue, I stressed the urgency of getting the work done. Still, Cedric raised no objections.

I raised the issue of payment but he implied that wouldn't be a problem. A relief for me because, although I knew he had a couple of thousand pounds under his bed, I also knew that some recluses could be very paranoid about money. They suffered from an irrational anxiety which bore no relation to their actual financial circumstances.

But Cedric seemed confident he could pay the bills for whatever needed doing in the house. He seemed also to recognize the necessity of the work being done.

Or at least that's how he seemed while the social workers were there as witnesses.

I was to discover a different attitude when he was dealing just with me.

Cedric Waites wasn't the first client with whom I'd encountered this particular problem. The problem of an unwillingness to open the door.

Wanting to get on with the job before he changed his mind, I had arranged to be back at the house at ten o'clock the following morning, the Tuesday. Until he got the police padlock removed and the front door lock replaced (another repair that would involve the intrusion of a workman), he proposed that I should knock on the back door.

Which of course I did. On the dot of ten. And received no response.

As I say, I'd been here before. Whatever a recluse or hoarder may agree to do, the instinct to bar access to their domain is a strong and enduring one.

I gave it half an hour that first day. Kept knocking. Also calling out. I've had clients whose fears of getting complaints from the neighbours, or of drawing attention to their reclusive behaviour, have been more powerful than their fear of intrusion into their homes.

It didn't work with Cedric Waites. Not that day.

Nor the next day.

Nor the one after.

I stayed there half an hour each time. That's what I'd learned to do. Just the half-hour. He wasn't going anywhere. And I had other jobs to get on with. I couldn't put everything on hold for Cedric Waites.

I didn't want to resort to calling back the social workers. Or the police. Whether the latter could do anything was a grey area, anyway. Whether they would do anything was equally uncertain. Besides, I had my professional pride. Over the years I had winkled plenty of recalcitrant creatures out of their shells. It was a matter of patience. One of us would get bored with the game first. I just had to ensure it wasn't me.

Of course, I still had my copy of the back door key. Some people might have thought that was the obvious solution. An old man like Cedric wasn't going to manhandle me out of his house, was he?

But experience of such cases told me that wouldn't work. If we were going to make any progress, it had to be the client's initiative that got me inside. There had to be some tiny level of complicity.

I got a minor breakthrough on the Thursday, in that Cedric did actually appear behind the glass panel of the back door and spoke to me. I shouted back that I couldn't hear what he was saying (which was almost true), and he went as far as to half-open an adjacent kitchen window.

'Go away.' It was not said in anger, more as if I were a wearisome inconvenience that he had to deal with. 'You know I'm not going to let you in.'

'I know,' I said with more confidence than I felt, 'that you are going to let me in . . . eventually. So why not cut to the chase and let me in now?'

'My dear Ellen,' he said – at least he had taken my name in, 'I am not going to let you in. You will have a long wait for "eventually". In fact, it'll be "over my dead body" . . . which I believe is how the police were expecting to step when they broke in here last week.'

So, he had a sense of humour. Good. I smiled at his little joke. Smiles are bonding. It's more difficult to be adversarial when people smile at you. '"Eventually" will come,' I said.

'Oh yes? I'm in my own house. I'm not breaking any laws. If I don't want to come out, nobody can get me out.'

'They could if there was a health-and-safety issue.'

'There is no health-and-safety issue.'

'No? There's something wrong with your central heating boiler. Suppose there was a gas leak from it? Suppose, when I was in the house yesterday, I smelt gas?'

'You wouldn't have smelt gas. Natural gas has no smell. You would have smelt the odorant – usually mercaptan – which is added to natural gas for safety reasons.'

So, a bit of a pedant, too. This was useful to me. The more I found out about Cedric Waites, the more points of contact I might have with him, details I could engage with.

'Anyway,' he went on, 'you didn't smell any gas yesterday. If there had been a gas leak in the house, I would have smelt it.'

'Maybe. I was just offering a hypothetical scenario. If there were gas leaking and it mixed with air and there was a spark from a light switch or—'

'I'm not very interested in hypothetical scenarios.'

'All I'm saying is that, if there were a gas explosion in your house, it would not just affect you. It might well destroy the houses either side as well. None of us is responsible only for our own safety.'

'Oh, very good,' he said. 'The "John Donne Defence", is that it? "No man is an island, entire of itself"? Is that the point you're trying, rather clumsily, to get across to me?'

Literary, too. I grinned and replied, 'If you like. See you tomorrow,' I added, as I made my way back to the front of the house.

He called after me, 'Not if I see you first!'

Banter. I was getting somewhere.

Suffice to say that, the next morning, Cedric let me into the kitchen.

Though very defensive, he was polite. And coherent. I had got that impression at our previous meeting, but experience of other clients' behaviour had made me wary of assuming complete sanity in anyone until I had proof of it.

Cedric Waites, though, seemed aware of the realities of his

situation. Allowing his household amenities to fall apart around him any further could prove a danger not only to himself but also to his neighbours. And facing another winter without central heating was not an appealing prospect. He seemed a little embarrassed by the situation in which he found himself.

That first morning he let me in, he offered me a cup of coffee. I declined, on the basis I'd just had one (I hadn't). I was deterred by the state of his kitchen.

Talking to Cedric, it soon became clear what had triggered his reclusiveness. A bereavement. It very often is. He had worked as a solicitor in the charity sector and his wife Felicity (whom he – and everyone else, it seemed – called Flick) had been a practice nurse at the local GPs' surgery. Their one child, Roy, had been off their hands for a long time, nearly fifty, married and settled in Worcester. So, Cedric and Flick had engineered their retirements to coincide and looked forward to fitting in the more extensive foreign travel that their working lives had prevented them from enjoying up until that point. All set fair.

Then, eight years previously, within a month of retirement, Flick had been found to have pancreatic cancer. It had been sudden and savage and killed her less six weeks after diagnosis.

That's what had started it. Cedric had coped with the funeral as well as could be expected of him. Son Roy and his wife Michelle had come down from Worcester for a few days to settle him back into the empty 14 Seacrest Avenue. They hadn't stayed long. Though they didn't have a lot in common, Roy got on all right with his father. But Michelle had never bonded with the old man. It was a relief to all three when the couple returned to Worcester (Michelle having made some specious excuse about needing 'to get back to the garden' – she was very keen on her garden).

There was something their friends and neighbours had never noticed about the Waites's marriage. It's quite common when you know a couple well that you cease to be aware of the dynamic between them. Flick had been recognized to be chatty and easy to get along with, Cedric quieter but perfectly amiable. And no one really considered the fact that it was she who had initiated all of their social life. As a result, with Flick off the scene, it was all too easy to forget that Cedric was left on his own. Had he been the partner who had died, everyone would have been all over Flick with care and condolence. But, because it was Cedric, it was easy to forget about him.

As it turned out, this lack of interest from their former social circle suited Cedric Waites very well. Perhaps he'd never had much need of company, but in bereavement that tendency became more pronounced. He told me he went through an initial stage of accepting invitations from well-wishing friends, then the realization that he really didn't want to accept them, followed by a feeling of great relief when he refused everything. Starved of response, the invitations soon dried up completely. And Cedric became more and more confirmed in his reclusiveness.

This process, of course, took place over months and years. He vouchsafed me details gradually during the period that I visited him. Which was a long time.

(I often think it's just as well that I run SpaceWoman on my own. If I had a partner with a grain of financial sense, they would undoubtedly point out to me how much valuable time I spent visiting clients who were no longer paying for my services. All right, I know. There's no commercial logic there. But my besetting fault is that I get interested in people and I want to see how their stories turn out.)

The trust built slowly. Having been finally admitted after nearly a week of doorstepping, I took a risk and told Cedric that I would return exactly seven days later, again on the Friday, to start clearing the food containers. When I arrived for the appointment, I fully expected him to have blocked me out again.

But no. He let me in. Granted, he watched me very closely as I packed away the ancient plastic into binbags. But he didn't interfere or comment on what I was doing. And he agreed when I suggested that I should bring my heating engineer Dean along the next week to see what could be done about the boiler.

So, there built up between us something that could almost be called a relationship. Dean started work on the boiler replacement and Cedric agreed to let him in each morning for the duration of the job. Dean also applied his plumbing skills to sealing the leak from the upstairs lavatory. But a quick look at the state of the staircase showed evidence of rot from the seeping water. It was a specialist job for a carpenter.

I knew the right person for that job too, someone rather closer to me than the other workmen. His name began with a 'D', too. Dodge. I'd met him when I realized that SpaceWoman was going to need the services of a driver to transport the various forms of clutter that the job threw up. From being a City whizz-kid, Dodge, following some kind of breakdown, had become an avid anti-consumerist and recycler, chiefly of wooden pallets. Though there are vast areas of his personality I don't know, I hope he thinks of me as a friend.

Dodge has his own reclusive tendencies, too, so he pretty soon settled into the rituals of 14 Seacrest Avenue. He also shared some of his foraged vegetarian meals with the old man and sometimes brought single-portion meals for the freezer. I don't know whether he and Cedric talked when I wasn't there – they certainly didn't when I was – but I like to feel they were at ease in each other's company.

I know that Cedric felt increasingly at ease in my company. Occasionally, when I'd over-catered for me and my son Ben, I might bring portions of meals for him. After initial reluctance, followed by insistence that he should pay me for the food, he came to accept my charity. Trust had reached the unexpected level of Cedric giving me a copy of the back door key to let myself in.

So, that was the set-up: central heating back working, Dodge returning to do minor maintenance jobs when required, me having got into the habit of paying a quick visit once a week . . . until that Friday morning when I let myself in and found Cedric dead.

TWO

He was on the bed, not in it. He hadn't been there long. Dodge, I found out later, had been in on the Thursday and Cedric had been fine then.

There was vomit around the dead man's mouth and on the duvet cover. Perhaps he'd choked on something.

I felt very sad about the death, but not desolated. I'd enjoyed the time I'd spent with Cedric, the way I had got to know him better, but I knew his life would never recapture the serenity he seemed to have shared with Flick. And he was well into his seventies. Perhaps a quick departure was a blessing.

I took the appropriate steps. Before anything else, I found Roy Waites's phone number and let him know what had happened. Then I contacted the police.

They asked me to stay on the premises until they arrived, which I dutifully did.

I think I was in shock. I had seen dead bodies before, but the finality of death never loses its power to traumatize. The fact that, only a week before, Cedric Waites had been part of my life – not a major part but a factor in it – and now he longer existed. As I say, I was in shock.

I think that was why my congenital inability to do nothing – and perhaps a feeling that the neatness of the house was a tribute to my services – led me to tidy up the few things that were littered about. Newspapers – getting them delivered again had been another sign of Cedric's progress – and, once more, a few food containers. I noticed that none of them was shop-bought. They were all plastic storage boxes which had stored meals cooked for Cedric by friends or neighbours. I thought that was kind of wistfully encouraging, suggesting that in his last months he had been building up more social contact.

Since I wasn't sure whether 14 Seacrest Avenue was back on the refuse collectors' radar, by force of habit I collected the containers up and put them in the back of the Yeti, my bargain-basement Skoda SUV, to be disposed of on the next of my regular visits to the dump. (I tend to wait until the boot space is full and then unload the lot at the Chichester Recycling Centre in Westhampnett.)

The police, when they turned up, inspected the body, asked me some fairly predictable questions, took my contact details, and said I could get on with my day. So far as they were concerned, just one less geriatric in Chichester. They clearly had no suspicion of criminal activity.

I had a final farewell moment with Cedric's body before it was taken away, and left 14 Seacrest Avenue for, I thought, the last time.

I had other clients to deal with.

Mim Galbraith was one, whose case was sadly typical. She had been head of English at a private girls' school in Petersfield. I got the impression, from things she said to me, that she had been a teacher rather in the Jean Brodie mould, an adventurous maverick disapproved of by the rest of the staff and worshipped by her pupils.

Mim had not regarded education as something that should be confined to the classroom. She would take any excuse to get her charges on trips to museums and theatre shows. She believed strongly that an appreciation of Jane Austen would be enhanced by a visit to the writer's house at Chawton, and that Kipling's loyalty to the tradition of British history was better understood after seeing his home, Bateman's, in the Sussex Weald. There were excursions to readings by then unknown poets held in dingy Charing Cross Road bookshops.

Mim was equally keen on foreign trips. What a tour of the chateaux of the Loire had to do with English literature was a question never asked by her enthusiastic pupils – or their parents who were footing the bills. Nor did anyone wonder about the relevance of three days spent walking the Camino de Santiago, the Spanish pilgrim route to the shrine of St James the Great in Galicia. Mim's pupils were having their horizons broadened, they were being made aware of the wider possibilities of life. That was what mattered.

Maybe, if I'd had a charismatic teacher in that mould, I might have been motivated to go to university. I'd always liked literature and reading. My A-level results were good enough to get me a place somewhere. But when I left school, I thought I'd had enough education for a while, so I took local jobs – waitressing, bar work and so on – for a while, and then travelled. America, North and South. Australia, where a relationship with the wrong man took the best part of four years out of my life. Applying to university when I returned to Chichester after that seemed irrelevant. I had moved on.

Then I got married to Oliver, the children followed, and thoughts of further education were gone for good.

I gathered from Mim that, towards the end of her career, she rather fell out of love with teaching. The management grew more authoritarian, less keen on extra-curricular activities. The foreign expeditions had been curtailed and eventually stopped. New health-and-safety regulations, new concerns about what teenage girls might get up to when monitored only by an ageing woman, had effectively clipped her wings. I got the impression that, by the time Mim retired, she was regarded by her younger colleagues as an eccentric relic from another age. And she was glad to leave a profession which had changed irrevocably from the one that had held such allure for her as a young woman.

In her prime, though (another Jean Brodie reference), Mim's lessons must have been riveting and inspiring. Her passion for English literature was undimmed in old age, but sadly her memory for the names of writers and quotations from their works often failed.

Apparently as adventurous in her private life as in the professional one, she had mixed with the emerging poets of her generation and had many lovers over the years. But such free spirits can end up alone in old age, and that had been Mim's fate. As they grew older, her old flames either guttered out terminally or settled for the warmth of a monogamous domestic hearth. There was no room in their lives for lovers. For so long an object of admiration, the relentless pressure of years had transformed Mim into the last thing she ever wanted to be, an object of pity.

And, cruelly, the moths of dementia had started to pick holes in the fine fabric of her brain.

*   *   *

The first time I encountered Mim Galbraith's name was in an email enquiry on the SpaceWoman website. Not from her. Like so many of my clients, she was totally unaware that she had a need of decluttering services.

No, the message came from an ex-pupil of hers called Allegra Cramond. When I called back, I was greeted by a no-nonsense woman with patrician vowels, which somehow seemed to be in keeping with her name. I later found out that she had spent most of her working life abroad in various Foreign Office postings. Unmarried, on retirement she had returned to Midhurst in the West Sussex where she had been brought up. Once settled in, she began to make contact with old school friends who still lived in the area. And it was through them that she tracked down Mim Galbraith.

Achieving this had not been as easy as she had expected. Though devoted to her charges while she was teaching them, Mim had made little effort to keep in touch thereafter. Once one lot was off her hands, her interest moved on to the next intake.

Mim had been unwilling for Allegra to call at the house, but her ex-pupil, whose professional life had been spent dealing with the likes of Afghan warlords, was not one to take 'no' for an answer. Having found out the address, she had gone straight round to knock on the door. Her quarry's engrained politeness ensured that she was invited in.

'Frankly, what I saw inside appalled me,' said Allegra on that first phone call. 'I don't think Mim was ever the tidiest of people, but by then the place was a complete tip. I had to do something about it.'

'Which is why you're calling me?' I asked.

'You're not the first person I called.'

'Oh?'

'I got on to another decluttering service, who made a start on the house, but I'm afraid things didn't work out there.'

Though restricting myself to another non-committal 'Oh?', I was intrigued to know more. Simple professional interest. In work like mine, it's difficult to assess how the opposition's faring. And I would have loved to know why 'things didn't work out' with the other company. But it wasn't the moment to pursue that line of enquiry.

Allegra Cramond assessed my prices in a professional manner

and didn't seem to find them excessive. 'I don't think Mim's hard up,' she said, 'though living in that huge house is financially impractical. Mind you, I wouldn't be the one to suggest she should move.' So, her pushiness had its limits. 'She'll pay you readily enough once I persuade her that the job needs doing. Or, if she doesn't, I will.'

Fine by me. So long as my bills get paid, I don't mind too much who's paying them.

'So,' my new client went on, 'let's fix a time when we can visit Mim together.'

'Are you sure she'll welcome the intrusion?'

'I'm sure she won't. But I'm equally sure that I will be able to convince her of the necessity.'

Allegra Cramond was back where she liked to be, in control.

Mim Galbraith didn't make any pretence that she welcomed my presence in her house. The place was, as Allegra had suggested, far too large for one elderly woman. Three storeys high, on the edge of farmland, it had, I later discovered, been owned by Mim's parents. The rooms had high ceilings and must have been ruinous to heat. There were also too many stairs for a woman in her nineties to negotiate safely.

Though she had spent much of her young adulthood dossing on friends' floors in London, the Midhurst house had been her primary residence all her life. (Apparently, her daily commute from there to Petersfield in a red two-seater MG TC Midget also contributed to her mythological status amongst her pupils.)

Mim Galbraith was tall and angular with a froth of white hair. There seemed to be no layer of anything between her skin and bones, but she moved gracefully and it was possible to see the striking woman she had once been. Her voice had the clipped cadences of long-gone radio announcers.

Though I wasn't welcome, Mim was far too well brought up not to offer tea or coffee. From a professional point of view, my instinct is to say no. Stuff prepared in hoarders' kitchens is rarely to be recommended. My turning down refreshment in clients' homes has, I'm sure, spared me botulism on more than one occasion. But Allegra said she'd make the drinks, which made me feel safer.

Mim's problem, incidentally, was apparent the moment I entered the house. Not surprising perhaps for someone of her background, it was books. The hall was littered with them, and the sitting room into which Allegra and I were led was rendered virtually impassable. The shelves covering every wall had probably been custom-built in a previous generation but were now in an advanced state of dilapidation. Whether through their wood rotting or the burden of books placed on them, their original parallel formation had now subsided into a chaos of diagonals. Volumes had slid down the inclines and tumbled to the floor, some open, some torn, some wrenched from their bindings.

And the space was permeated by that distinctive musty smell produced by damp seeping through old paper and leather.

Though she had greeted Allegra, and offered drinks to both of us, Mim thereafter behaved as if I wasn't there. She didn't respond when I was introduced by name. It was only once we were all seated in dusty armchairs (from two of which piles of books had had to be removed) that she looked directly at me and demanded, 'Do you like books?'

'Yes,' I was able to reply with complete honesty. 'I don't get as much time for reading as I'd like but I'm one of those people who daren't go on public transport without a book in my bag – and indeed an emergency book in case there are delays and I finish the first one.'

'Hm,' was all Mim Galbraith said. But the 'Hm' made it just over the edge into approval. Still transfixing me with her eyes, she said, 'The other people didn't like books. All they wanted me to do was to get rid of books.'

'I certainly wouldn't want to do that. Or at least I wouldn't want to get rid of any books you didn't want to get rid of.'

'I don't want to get rid of any books,' said Mim combatively. 'All of my books have sentimental associations.'

'That's fine then,' I said. 'But maybe I could help bring some order into your books.' I gestured to the walls. 'Mend some of the shelves, perhaps . . .?'

'Do you mend shelves?' asked Mim. 'The other people didn't mend shelves.'

'I wouldn't claim to be an expert carpenter, but I have mended a good few shelves in my time. It's part of the job.'

'And what is the job? What do you call yourself?'

'A "declutterer".'

'Mm.' She assessed my answer for a moment. 'Ugly word, isn't it?'

'I agree. Wish there was a better one. But it does at least describe what it's meant to describe.'

'Yes. The English language is full of words like that. Squat, functional words. Do you know, I heard a person on the wireless once describe themselves as a "scent-maker". The French *"parfumier"* is so much more elegant.'

'I would agree.'

'And then there's "tailor". Such a dull, blunt English word. How much nicer is . . . is . . .' But the French wouldn't come.

This was clearly a linguistic riff Allegra had heard before, because she supplied, *'"Couturier".'*

'I know, I know!' Mim responded tetchily. But clearly she didn't.

That was just the first of the times she lost her thread. It was painful. Clearly a woman of high intelligence, used to queening it in conversation, she visibly hated being let down by a defective memory.

For the first few blips, Allegra again supplied the word that had been lost, but this patently angered Mim, so then we focused on the practicalities of how I might be able to help her.

With Allegra leading – a role that came naturally to her – we at last agreed that I should come to the house the following Monday morning with my toolkit and check out the damage to the shelves. If it was just a case of replacing a few Rawlplugs that had come out, then I could do that. If, on the other hand, whole shelves needed replacing, it'd be an expert's job. And I had just such an expert in mind. Dodge again, whose driving skills and 1951 Morris Commer CV9/40 Tipper van I always engaged when I had a major clutter disposal problem. His carpentry skills were unrivalled.

But that morning I didn't mention the possibility of using Dodge. I knew the minds of hoarders too well. Mim Galbraith was uncomfortable enough with the idea of letting one person, me, into her house again. I didn't want to frighten her off by suggesting a second visitor.

Allegra had clearly organized appointments for her former teacher before. She wrote my visit into a large desk diary which lay, amidst a pile of other books, on a table beside Mim's armchair. After that, she checked a wall calendar over the fireplace.

'You haven't been crossing the days off, Mim,' she said reprovingly. 'If you do that last thing at night, like I told you, then you'll always know what day it is the next morning.'

The old lady appeared not to hear this. Or maybe she deliberately ignored Allegra when she got bossy. Instead, she looked at me with sudden beadiness.

'Do you live on your own?' she asked.

'Yes,' I replied. It was pretty much true. My son Ben, who'd been in residence for a while, was now spending most of his time at his girlfriend's place.

'So, you're a spinster too?' said Mim.

I didn't deny it. Too complicated to go into the business of being a widow and how Oliver had died. Easier to let it go.

'Now that's a word I do like,' Mim pronounced. '"Spinster". It's had a bad press, but I've never minded being called it. One who spins . . . and who knows what we spin? Stories, dreams, fantasies . . .? I always loved Sylvia Plath's poem, "Spinster". Have you read it, Ellen?'

The first time she had used my name. She was much more focused than she had been earlier in the conversation.

'I have read it,' I replied truthfully. Like many teenage girls, I'd gone through a self-questioning Sylvia Plath stage. 'But not for a long time.'

'I love it,' said Mim, and I could feel the enthusiasm which had communicated itself to so many of her pupils. 'I was contemporary with Ted at Cambridge, and then I saw him and Sylvia a bit, back when they were living in Primrose Hill. Lovely poem, though, "Spinster". It begins . . .' She dredged her memory for a moment. 'And there's this great line about a snowflake . . .'

But the instant recollection of quotations, which Allegra had mentioned to me, failed Mim. I could see the anguish that her inability to remember the lines caused her.

'Don't worry,' she said hastily, fearing perhaps that Allegra was about to recite the poem. 'I've got a copy. It's in *The Colossus and Other Poems*, on the shelf over there.'

She sprang from her armchair to get the book that would save her embarrassment.

She couldn't find it.

As I've implied, I'm always dealing with a variety of clients at different stages of their decluttering journey. Some problems are sorted with one visit, others drag on for weeks and months (and I'm not including the unpaid aftercare for people like Cedric, which can stretch into years).

The afternoon of the Friday I'd found the body at 14 Seacrest Avenue, I had an appointment with a new client. And, though I was a bit shaken by Cedric's death, I could see no good reason to postpone the meeting. Life contained one less person, who I'd known and liked, but it still had to go on.

It was the wife who'd contacted me. Lita, Lita Cullingford. She'd sounded breathy and enthusiastic on the phone. And it was soon clear that her principles were very green.

'What I'm keen to do,' she breathed, 'is to adapt our garage so that we can install a charging point for an electric car.'

'Very good idea,' I'd said, 'though I don't quite see why you would need my services to do that.'

'What do you mean? You do decluttering, don't you?'

'Yes. But I don't install charging points.'

'No. But the garage needs decluttering to make room for the charging point. And the electric car, come to that.'

'Do you mean decluttering? Or do you just mean clearing? Rubbish taken to the tip?'

'No, because it's not all just rubbish. Some of it's stuff that needs to go to a good home.'

Ah. This was more up my street. We fixed that I would go and check out the garage.

Which was the appointment I was going to at two o'clock in the afternoon of the day I found Cedric Waites's body.

Lita Cullingford. was small, dumpy, and earnest about saving the planet.

Her kitchen was immaculate, so I accepted the mint tea she offered me. It was made from leaves freshly plucked from a bush outside the kitchen door.

I didn't get a chance to say much, as she expatiated on her values and the need for recycling of everything. She was actually preaching to the converted here. Though I don't cram my principles down people's throats, I do sympathize with a lot of what she was saying. My immediate thought was that I should introduce her to Dodge. The two of them would certainly be singing from the same song sheet.

The house, in Halnaker, was well-appointed. Saving the planet, while clearly important, was not going to be allowed to inhibit the Cullingfords' lifestyle. I got the feeling that the electric car, when they bought it, would not be the cheapest on the market.

Lita took me through to the garage. I'd seen worse. Very much worse. There were a lot of dusty cardboard boxes. 'Full of rubbish,' Lita said. 'They just need chucking.'

With her permission, I looked inside a couple. Beaten-up chisels and saws, some battered power tools. Not in pristine condition, but no worse than the contents of most domestic toolboxes. Certainly still usable.

'Am I guilty of gender stereotyping,' I asked, 'if I were to suggest that most of this belongs to your husband?'

'No. You'd be right. It's Gerry's.'

'So, the garage is his "man cave"?'

'It's just where he keeps his stuff.'

'OK.' Experience has taught me to tread warily about such areas. 'And . . . Gerry . . . is happy for all this stuff to be got rid of?'

'Yes. He fully buys into the green agenda. It was he who first suggested getting the electric car.'

'Fine.' I looked further round the garage. Less dusty than the boxes, suggesting more recent use, was a set of golf clubs on a trolley. I know nothing about the game but, seeing the spec of all the other Cullingford possessions, I would assume they had cost a lot. Well used now, but originally expensive.

I chuckled. 'Presumably Gerry doesn't want me to get rid of those?'

'Oh, but he does. As I say, he's really seen the light as far as the green agenda's concerned. He's turned right against golf, you know, because of the harm it causes to the environment . . . the land clearance involved in building the courses, the amount of water that's used to keep the greens green. No, he doesn't want to have any more to do with the game.'

'OK.' I shrugged. 'Do you want me to see if I can get a buyer for them somewhere?'

'We'd prefer it if they could go to charity.'

For the first time, Lita Cullingford had my attention. I'd been about to turn down the job she was offering me. It was just clearance, not decluttering. She or her husband could sort out the problem with a couple of trips down to the municipal dump. They didn't need my services.

But now she'd mentioned charity, I felt differently. There was one particular charity that I knew which would really welcome a set of golf clubs

I'd got my electric blue SpaceWoman Yeti parked on the Cullingfords' drive and agreed to load up the stuff straight away. With the seats down, there was room to get it all in. We agreed I'd send an invoice for one hour of my time.

Lita and I parted on good terms, both very pleased with what we'd achieved.

I had a regular slot booked at the dump for the following morning. I'd get rid of the boxes and their contents then.

I drove straight from Halnaker to the Terminus Estate in Chichester. I have an encyclopedic knowledge of the local charities, can sort out the ones which actually do people good, from the ones which just provide platforms for rich women to boss other rich women around. And I knew an excellent charity run by a guy called Grant.

Basically, he and a dedicated team used sport to distract deprived local teenagers – mostly but not exclusively boys – from getting involved in drugs and gangs.

As I anticipated, he was delighted to have the donation of a decent set of golf clubs. I knew it'd be put to good use.

So, as I returned home, I felt good and rewarded myself with a large glass of Merlot.

The sadness and shock of finding Cedric Waites dead had been alleviated by the serendipity of having organized a good deed.

THREE

More basic information. Like I said, I'm a widow. I was married to Oliver, a successful cartoonist, and we had two children, Juliet (who now calls herself Jools) and Ben.

Oliver committed suicide. I still get a mild shock when I say that. It sounds so bald. Is it better if I say that Oliver was a lifelong depressive and the illness finally caught up with him?

Obviously, his death had a profound effect on my life. The pain doesn't go away. I still miss him every day. Many people seem to think I should feel guilty about what happened but I don't. I feel regret. For a lot of things. For the fact that I wasn't at home to stop him when he took the final step. But I don't feel guilt.

Having watched him through any number of depressive episodes during our marriage, I knew the power of the disease. I think at times my presence made things better for him, the fact that I was still there when he came out of the darkness, the fact that I recognized him as the same person who had gone in.

And we did have some wonderfully happy times together. When he was on top of things, he was amazingly good company. Very funny. And silly, in the best sense of the word. Though his bleak moods made him question his feelings about everything, I never doubted that he loved me. And no one who had seen him with the kids could doubt his love for them too.

Inevitably, his death impacted them. Jools (then still Juliet) was at the stroppiest stage of adolescence. Her reaction was to shut herself off from everything, not allowing any emotion to be expressed. She still, now working in the instant fashion business in London, rarely allows her carapace of self-reliance to crack. As a mother, when I have room amongst other worries, I regret my lack of closeness to my daughter.

Ben, whose age was still in single figures when his father died, reacted differently. I think he was always going to inherit the depressive gene, but Oliver's suicide on the edge of Ben's teens exacerbated the problem. And, as Ben's moods grew more volatile with age, it was also a constant reminder to me of the potential dangers of depression. As a result, I will never feel entirely secure about my son's safety.

There have been times, I know, when Ben has contemplated ending his own life, even got as far as making plans. Many mothers would be delighted to see their sons emulating their fathers. In my special circumstances, that is something I never wish to think about.

But I speak only in terms of the depressive inheritance. Ben takes on other aspects of his father's character of which I heartily approve. For a start, he's also very funny. Though his natural tendency is towards solitude, in company he can be the centre of attention, keeping everyone entertained with his anecdotes and banter. But with Ben, just as it had been with his father, he is at his funniest when on the edge of a manic phase. That can be a warning sign that a deep gloom is about to settle over him.

He's also inherited his father's artistic talent. As a small child, there was nothing he liked better than drawing. In fact, one of the most potent images my mind's retained is of four-year-old Ben crouched on the sitting-room floor, his bottom sticking up in the air and his face close to the piece of paper on which he was working with his crayons. At such moments of concentration, he was, as Oliver had been, oblivious to the world around him. And like his father's, Ben's tongue would protrude slightly from his mouth in the effort of creation.

Even at that age, he had a sense of line. With a few, economical strokes, he could produce something which was instantly recognizable, that had shape and depth. All right, I'm his mother and mothers are notoriously biased about their children's abilities, but my view was endorsed by art teachers when he went to school. And Oliver, who could be a harsh critic, also recognized – and gloried in – our son's talent.

It was no surprise then that Ben went to Nottingham Trent University to study graphic art. In his time there, he grew increasingly interested in the business of animation. To my delight, he embarked on a film project based on one of Oliver's most successful strip cartoons, *Riq and Raq*.

Sadly though, the recurrence of his depressive illness, with what amounted to two major breakdowns, meant that Ben dropped out of Nottingham Trent and never finished his course. He came back to live with me in Chichester but kept saying he ought to get out and stand on his own two feet. Part of me agreed with him. Another part probably enjoyed having him around the house more than I should have done. Not only was he engaging company, he was also somewhere where I could keep an eye on him, watching for the signs of his illness returning.

Ben's in a better place now . . . well, emotionally at least. After a confidence-crushing break-up with his university girlfriend Tracey, he's in a new relationship with a nurse called Pippa. She lives in Brighton and he spends more time at her place than he does with me.

I have to confess I'm not completely convinced she's the right woman for him. For someone in a caring profession, her manner can at times be quite insensitive. I wonder whether she's actually seen Ben in one of his deep depressions and how she would cope if she did. I can't see Pippa doing what many women do in such circumstances and blaming themselves. I'm not saying that's a good reaction, but I can't somehow see Pippa blaming herself for anything. Sorry, bitchy remark.

I know I must curb these thoughts. My son is in a relationship which seems to be making him happy. That's all I should care about. I also know I'm hypersensitive and over-protective because of what happened with Oliver. And yes, if I'm completely honest with myself, there could well be an element of maternal jealousy too. I never saw myself as the kind of mother who thought no woman was good enough for her son, but maybe I do have some element of that in me.

And I've never felt the empathy with Pippa that I experienced on my one brief meeting with Tracey.

Workwise, things may also be coming good for Ben. Since he returned from Nottingham to live with me in Chichester, he's been in the Walberton workshop, painting designs on the wonderful furniture that Dodge makes from recycled material, mostly old pallets.

The two of them get on well and what they produce is stunning. But I've never thought the collaboration was destined to work in the long term. They don't have artistic differences – they admire and respect each other's skills – but their attitudes to the commercial world are far apart. Dodge, whose real name is Gervaise, used to have a high-powered job in the City, but some kind of breakdown he suffered in his late twenties turned him totally against consumerism. He takes huge pride in the quality of the furniture he creates but wants to give it all to charitable causes. He is strongly opposed to the idea of making money from it.

Ben's attitude could not be more different. He's not by nature grasping but he does believe in being paid for his work. This is partly because he feels he should be contributing something to my domestic expenses, but with him it's also a matter of principle. Oliver was just the same. He valued his creativity and, unless he had agreed to do something for charity (which he frequently did), expected to be paid for it.

So, at the moment, Ben is working with Dodge, unpaid, and honing his skills in interior décor. But the situation can't last, and I don't think my son wants to be making furniture for the rest of his life. Somehow, he seems to be aware of how Oliver would have felt, that furniture design is a skill rather than an art. And that his son ought to be directing his talents into a more creative area.

Even there, though, a chink of light is appearing. I had rather assumed that the *Riq and Raq* animation project had ended with Ben's career at Nottingham Trent, but discovered recently that he has been continuing with it. While he was living here with me, he would spend hours up in his bedroom working on his laptop and I never asked what he was doing there. (That's a prohibition that all nosy mums of grown-up children have to abide by nowadays. Computers are private areas. You must wait till – if ever – such information is volunteered.)

Well, in this case, to my surprise, Ben did actually tell me what he'd been doing. He had completed the *Riq and Raq* animation. My obvious hope was that he'd then show it to me. But he didn't. He apologized but said he didn't want me to see it till he'd got some 'validation' from some 'mates'. Quite what that meant, I'm not sure. I know he's still in touch with people who were on the Nottingham Trent course with him. Possibly even with one of the tutors; there's a name he's mentioned. Maybe those are the 'mates' he's talking about, mates with some expertise in the world of animation.

Next thing I hear, announced rather sheepishly by Ben, is that his film has been shortlisted for an award. At the TOCA Film Festival in Turin. I immediately ask when the festival is. Two months' time. And what does 'TOCA' stand for? He doesn't know. Does he want to attend? Because if he's got a problem about the cost, I could help him out with . . .

No, he doesn't want to attend. He probably won't win, anyway. Daft to go all the way to Turin only to be disappointed. I know he's deliberately downplaying his prospects. Basically, he's got a great charge from being shortlisted. That's part of the 'validation' he was looking for. It could open up all kinds of career possibilities. But Ben forces himself to curb his imagination. He doesn't want to tempt fate.

Still he doesn't offer to show me the film. It seems strange, but I'm not going to be offended by it. I've long ago given up trying to second-guess all of Ben's behaviour.

One thing he's asked me not to do is to mention anything about the TOCA shortlisting to my mother 'because I know she'll just go on about it, Ma'. (He started calling me 'Ma' in a tone of send-up – now it's become habitual.)

But I did know exactly what he'd meant. My mother 'going on about things'. Fleur Bonnier, that's her. If you're of a certain generation, the name might mean something to you. She acted in West End plays, had minor roles in minor English movies. No, I shouldn't say that. I should say that she was a successful actress (though she'd call herself an 'actor' now, of course). Sorry, I do find it remarkably easy to be rude about my mother. God knows she's given me cause to be over the years.

My father was a fellow actor of hers whom I only met once. And when her friends had stopped saying what a beautiful baby I was, and how 'brave' she was for bringing me up on her own, Fleur rather lost interest in me. Having a small child around inhibited her professional life – not to mention her somewhat rackety private one. I got used to being farmed out to a mixed bag of 'friends', whose resentment at being lumbered with me did not stay hidden for long. Fleur was always off in the theatre, or filming, or organizing another of her complicated love affairs.

Not the ideal pattern of motherhood. And one which I tried not to replicate in my upbringing of my own children. Which is why my lack of closeness to Jools sometimes troubles me so much. Particularly because Fleur constantly maintains that she and her granddaughter have such a 'great relationship'. I don't really believe this. When the two of them get together, they affect a kind of high-camp chit-chat which is nearer to theatrical dialogue than normal conversation. And which Fleur knows full well (and possibly Jools also knows) annoys me very much to listen to. (Though I never say anything. From childhood onward, I have resisted giving my mother the satisfaction of seeing me rise to her digs at me.)

So, anyway, there was no danger of me telling Fleur about Ben's shortlisting for the TOCA Award. I wouldn't actually have told anyone. Indeed, I was quite honoured that Ben had mentioned it to me. There was a routine Oliver and I had followed whenever he was up for an award. Don't tell anyone. All right, if they found out about it through the media, there was nothing you could do about that. But our principle was: the fewer people know about the shortlist, the fewer people have to go through the agony of waiting for the announcement of the winner.

It worked well for us. Because Oliver did pick up a few awards in the course of his career. And cartoon awards don't have the all-media-conquering profile of something like the Oscars. So, often the only people who knew he'd been nominated were: Oliver himself, me, his agent and the editor of the cartoon section where the strip had appeared. If he won, we could then announce the triumph to everyone else. And if he lost, very few people even knew he had been shortlisted. Good scheme, huh?

It only struck me on the Saturday that there was one person who I should tell about Cedric Waites's death. And that was Dodge. He'd finished rebuilding the staircase some months before but had been back at 14 Seacrest Avenue during that week to replace a few rotten floorboards in the hall.

As ever, he'd not spent anything on materials. Dodge owned

a house near Walberton. He didn't live in it, he actually lived in one of the outbuildings. But the house was a repository for, as well as his completed furniture, all the stuff he'd scavenged and repossessed from skips. Needless to say, he had quite a choice of recyclable floorboards.

Dodge sounded guarded when he answered the phone that Saturday morning. I was used to that. I don't know precisely what all his demons were, but something had made his default position one of suspicion. I do know that his evasive telephone manner had put off more than one potential client for his 'TREASURES ON EARTH' recycling business. But he always relaxed when I identified myself.

'Oh, Ellen. Hello.' His private school vowels were at odds with his permanently scruffy appearance. 'Everything all right with you?' Said with a note of anxiety.

'Yes. Fine. Or at least I'm fine.'

'Oh.' More anxiety. 'Is there something wrong with Ben?' I doubt whether my son ever spoke to him about it, but Dodge seemed to have an instinctive empathy with his mental frailty. Maybe identifying it with his own.

'No, no. But I do have some sad news.' And I told him about Cedric's death.

'Oh, God. But he was fine when I left his place on Thursday.'

'Well, that's a good thing.'

'How?'

'It means he didn't suffer for long. His death must have been relatively quick.'

'I hope so.' Dodge was silent. Then he said, 'He was a good man. I'm sorry he's gone.'

'Yes. I think I was beginning to get through to him in the last few months.'

'We chatted a bit,' said Dodge.

This was an incongruous idea. Dodge's strange manner – autism or whatever it was – did not chime in with the idea of 'chatting'. But maybe he relaxed with people in whom he recognized another kind of mental stress. As he did with Ben. And I could imagine that their shared reclusiveness might have brought Dodge and Cedric together. I was possibly too normal to get through to him on that level.

Dodge went on, 'I was trying to persuade him about the benefits of vegetarianism.'

'Successfully?'

'I cooked him some veggie stuff. He wasn't that rude about it. Said it would have gone well with a good steak.' The idea clearly amused him but he didn't laugh. I tried to think if I'd ever heard Dodge laugh.

I chuckled.

'Do you know what he died of?'

'No. It looked like he might have choked on something but I'm not an expert. I assume the post mortem will find out the cause of death.'

'Post mortem? Will there have to be a post mortem?'

'Dodge, of course there will. The coroner has to be informed if the deceased hasn't been seen by a doctor within a fortnight. Cedric hadn't left his house or let anyone in for nearly ten years.'

'Hm. So there will be a post mortem?'

'The police seemed to think there definitely would be.'

'The police? Why were the police involved?'

Dodge sounded seriously alarmed. I reminded myself that he'd reacted like that before. He was profoundly unwilling to have anything to do with the police. I don't know for certain, but I think drugs were involved at some level in Dodge's major break-down. He certainly now acts as a volunteer in some kind of drug rehabilitation programme. Whether he fell foul of the police because of that . . . as I say, I really don't know.

I tried to calm him down, telling him that no one could think he had any involvement in the death of Cedric Waites.

'No?' said Dodge. 'But it sounds like I was the last person to see him alive.'

'Have you heard from Jools recently?' Fleur drawled.

She was round at my place. I had cooked Sunday lunch. For just the two of us. Never my favourite configuration of personnel.

But on the phone she'd sounded pathetic, as only she can sound pathetic. Not for nothing was she an actress. Her husband Kenneth was playing in a golf tournament and so Fleur would be 'on my little ownsome'.

I'd swallowed the bait and offered her lunch. Also, knowing

how much she was likely to drink, I had said I'd pick her up and take her back to her place. Not only would that enable me to resist her encouragements for me to drink as much as she did, it would give me some control over how long the lunch lasted. It would also quite possibly save other road-users from my mother's erratic post-prandial driving.

'No,' I replied to her enquiry about Jools. Then, anticipating the cooing ritual about how the two of them were 'just girls together', I asked, 'Have you?'

But all I got was, 'No. No, I haven't. Not recently. She must be busy with all her product launches and catwalk shows.'

'Probably,' I said, my tone a little dry.

And, of course, then Fleur couldn't resist adding, 'Oh, but we'll have such giggles when we do make contact again!'

'I'm sure you will.'

'And Ben? How's Ben?'

'Fine. In Brighton with Pippa.'

'Oh yes.' My mother's acting training enabled her to get a lot of nuance into those two words. 'And you've met this one, haven't you?'

'I have, yes.'

She couldn't resist the dig. 'Whereas Ben never introduced you to that Tracey, did he?'

'No.' It was true. And I wasn't about to tell Fleur that Tracey had sought me out and we had actually met.

'Hm. He hasn't introduced this Pippa to me.' It was a remark that didn't need any comment, so I didn't give any. 'Do you think he's ashamed of me?'

'I would just think that Ben and Pippa enjoy spending time together more than they do with other people,' I replied neutrally.

'Hm. Odd. You'd think he'd want her to meet the famous one in the family.'

Just when I think I'll never hear a more extreme example of my mother's self-centredness, she'll come up with something like that. I was lost for words.

Not that anyone's loss of words was ever going to derail Fleur Bonnier from the course on which she had set out. 'And Ben's all right, is he?'

'He's fine.'

'You know what I mean?'

'Yes, of course I know what you mean.'

But she still felt the need to spell it out. 'I was talking about his mental health.'

'I know you were, Fleur.' My mother has always insisted that I call her by her first name. Maybe she thinks it projects an image of us being girlie girls together. Something that Fleur and I never were and never will be. 'And you can rest assured that Ben is perfectly fine.'

Though, even as I said the words, I felt a pang of anxiety.

'Good. Well, I hope that continues.' Long practice stopped me from responding, from defending my son. So, Fleur moved on seamlessly to another time-tested line of attack. 'It's lucky that Jools hasn't inherited that bit of her father's personality.'

Better say nothing than unleash my instinctive response to that. Even though Oliver was nearly ten years dead, Fleur could still not resist wheeling out more implied criticism of him.

'She's doing very well, young Jools,' she went on. 'Becoming an influencer in the fashion world. She's got lots of followers. And her content gets lots of likes.' Showing her easy familiarity with the world of online marketing. Or – more probably – quoting verbatim from her granddaughter. 'I'm glad she's making a mark in the world of glamour. Good that someone in the family is following in my footsteps.'

I knew where Fleur was going with this and I gritted my teeth to stop myself from a knee-jerk reaction.

She resumed, 'Rather more exciting than being a cleaner.'

This was another old gibe, her deliberate refusal to acknowledge what the work of SpaceWoman actually was. And it always caught me on the raw. In fact, I might well have lashed back at her, had I not been saved by the landline ringing.

'Hello?'

'Is that Ellen Curtis?' A man's voice, deep, confident.

'Yes.'

'You don't know me. My name's Tim Goodrich, and I'm the executor of Cedric Waites's will.'

'Oh. Good afternoon.'

'I gather that you were the person who found him.'

'Yes.'

'I'm sorry. It must have been distressing for you.'

'A bit of a shock, yes. But I'm glad he seems to have died fairly quickly.'

'Yes. I am, obviously, rather interested in the details of how he died.'

'That's understandable.'

'I wonder, Ellen, would it be possible for us to meet?'

FOUR

'Roy – that's Cedric's son – and his wife Michelle will be arriving in Chichester from Worcester tomorrow,' said Tim Goodrich.

'Right. And how do you come to be the executor? Are you part of the family?'

'No. It's a rather strange connection, actually . . .'

It was that Sunday evening. We were sitting in a pub near the Market Cross in the centre of Chichester. It was, I only remembered once we had agreed to meet there, the one I'd gone to with Oliver the first time I met him. He'd come to do an author talk about one of his cartoon books in the Waterstones, where I was working at the time. Back then it was midwinter, Chichester had been dark and covered with snow. Now, at seven thirty in the evening, benefiting from the recent change to Summer Time, it was still daylight.

'I really knew his wife,' Tim continued, 'rather than Cedric himself.'

'Flick,' I said.

'Yes. Did you know her?'

'No, it was just that Cedric was always talking about Flick.'

'Yes, I'm sure he was. One of those marriages where he would have been totally helpless without her.'

'As he proved to be,' I said.

'Yes. Anyway, Flick was the one I knew. Or at least I met her first. I'm a doctor. She was one of the practice nurses when I was attached to a surgery here in Chichester. I got quite close to both of them. They were redoing their wills at some point and she asked if I'd mind being put down as Cedric's executor, the assumption being that he'd go before she did, she'd sort out his estate and my services wouldn't be called on much. But, as it turned out . . .'

'She went first.'

'Yes. Sad, she was a lovely woman. Life and soul of every party.'

He was pensive for a moment and took a long swallow from his pint of Harvey's. I was drinking Merlot. Could go for a second glass if the suggestion arose – I had walked from home.

It was the first opportunity I had really had to look at him. Tim Goodrich, fifties probably, round my age, trim but beginning to thicken out. Dark hair giving way to grey. And the voice that I'd noticed on the phone, mellow, reassuring. I could imagine that he'd been a very good doctor. A person one could confide in without embarrassment.

'You imply,' I said, 'that you're no longer working in Chichester.'

'No, I'm not. There were things I liked about being a GP, but I didn't really feel fulfilled doing it. And I had domestic problems, as well.' This intrigued me but I didn't say anything. 'So, I went back to Oxford to do a PhD. In fact, my leaving the practice coincided with Flick's retirement, so we had a joint farewell party. We're talking eight years ago now. In the George and Dragon in North Street – you probably know it?'

'Yes.'

'And then, only a few weeks later . . .' He ran out of words. It seemed that Cedric's wife had meant a lot to him.

I shifted the conversation. 'Are you still doing the PhD?'

'No, I got that. Stayed in Oxford, though. Doing research, which I think is where I always wanted to be.'

'And what are you doing research into?'

He chuckled. 'I don't want to blind you with science.'

'Try me,' I said.

'The subject of my research is serotonin. Heard of it?'

'Yes.' I wasn't going to say how I knew. 'Serotonin is the substance in the body whose levels can be adjusted by certain antidepressants.'

'Very good.' He nodded his head slowly up and down in an act of admiration. '"Selective serotonin reuptake inhibitors", to give them their full title. Well, even now we know relatively little about how serotonin works. That's what I'm trying to find out.'

'Good luck.'

'Thank you. We continue to need it.' He took another swallow of Harvey's. 'And you, Ellen? I gather you were at Cedric's house in a professional capacity . . .?'

'Yes.'

'So, what exactly do you do?'

I explained. And, bless him, he got it first time. None of this thinking I did house clearance or, if you were in my mother's camp, cleaning. Tim Goodrich understood what decluttering is, and also why there was such need for it in modern society.

'Do you know of other people round here who provide the same service?' asked Tim.

'Decluttering? I'm sure there are others. I've heard a few names mentioned, but I haven't had anything to do with them. I wouldn't, really. I work on my own.'

'Oh? Well, there is one locally who seems to have it in for you.'

'Really?' The idea seemed incongruous. Since I'd had no dealings with another declutterer, I'd given no one cause to take against me.

Tim explained. 'I heard from Roy that his father's body had been found by the declutterer who'd been working with him, so I thought I'd make contact. But Roy hadn't got your name.' I was slightly miffed by that; he might have registered who it was had rung to inform him of his father's death. But then again, he could have been distracted by the news and not taking things in properly. (I always try to think the best of people, though sometimes it's bloody hard work.)

'So, when I got down here,' Tim continued, 'I went online to check out declutterers. There weren't many. I tried the first one on the list, BrightHome. I asked the woman if she'd been doing some work at Fourteen Seacrest Avenue. She said no, that would probably be SpaceWoman. And then she said . . .' He hesitated.

'Then she said what?'

'"Steer clear of her, unless you want to get ripped off."'

'What!' Obviously, I've had complaints over the years I've been operating SpaceWoman. You can't run a business like mine without putting a few backs up. Also, I tend to be dealing with people at a stressful time of their lives when they're quick to take offence. But to know that there was someone out there deliberately badmouthing me and my work . . . well, it was a shock.

Tim apologized. 'I'm just reporting what she said. Is she someone you've had run-ins with before?'

'What's her name?'

'Rosemary Findlay.'

'Not only have I not had run-ins with her, I've never heard of her.'

'I'm sorry to have drawn her to your attention then.'

'No, Tim. If there's someone out there saying stuff like that about me, I'd rather know.' I shook my head in bewilderment. 'Very odd.'

'I would like you to rest assured,' said Tim, affecting a lawyer-like voice, 'that, having met you, I am convinced that Rosemary Findlay is an appallingly mendacious woman and everything she has said about you is vile calumny.'

I giggled. 'Oh well, thanks. That's very British of you.'

With a smile, he nodded his head, acknowledging the mock-compliment. 'I wonder if you'd mind, Ellen, just running through for me the precise circumstances of how you found Cedric's body. Now I'm stuck in this role of executor, I'd like to have as much information as possible.'

So, I went through the sequence of events, more or less exactly as I had for the police.

At the end, he thanked me and suggested another glass of Merlot. I hadn't noticed that my glass was nearly empty and readily agreed. As I say, no driving to worry about. Besides, I was enjoying Tim Goodrich's company.

He brought my drink and had got himself a second pint. 'I think we should raise a glass to Cedric's memory,' he said. We did, and both took long swallows.

Then, quite abruptly, Tim changed the subject. 'Silly question to ask, but you have no reason to think that there was anything odd about Cedric's death?'

'"Odd"? As in . . .?'

'"Odd", as in: Do you think he died a natural death?'

'Is death ever "natural"? Actually, I believe it is. I'm not religious or anything, but I do believe that there's a natural span to everyone's life. And, for Cedric, whose life had been so diminished by the loss of Flick, yes, I would say that he had reached the end of his natural span.'

'Hm.'

'You don't sound convinced.'

'No. It's silly. Just, when you know someone's medical history . . .'

'You were Cedric's GP?'

'Yes. And he was one of the ones I thought would last long into his nineties.'

'Maybe, Tim. But, even for a doctor, life expectancy isn't an exact science, is it?'

'True.'

'Flick was presumably expected to live way beyond retirement and yet she lasted only a couple of months.'

'Yes, yes, you're right.' He grinned wearily. 'This is the wrong way round. You should be the romantic sentimentalist. I should be the cold-eyed, scientific realist.'

'Well, you certainly know more about medical matters than I do.'

'I suppose I do.'

'Besides, however robust Cedric may have been when you last saw him, I can't think that eight years of solitary incarceration in Fourteen Seacrest Avenue was conducive to good health.'

'No. You're right.' Another long swallow of Harvey's. 'I can't get away from the feeling, though.'

'What feeling?'

'The feeling that there was something funny about Cedric's death.'

FIVE

I fixed to meet Tim at 14 Seacrest Avenue at two on the Monday afternoon. Roy and Michelle Waites were driving down from Worcester that morning and would be in Chichester by then.

The appointment fitted in well with my schedule. First thing, I'd go to the dump and unload the accumulation of stuff in the Yeti's boot. Then I could arrive, as agreed, at Mim Galbraith's house, with my toolkit, to see if I could mend her broken shelving.

I had worried that Mim might cancel at the last minute. On our first encounter, she hadn't welcomed my intrusion into her life. But no cancellation message arrived. Maybe Allegra Cramond had exercised her version of a three-line whip. And it would be a bold person who would cross her.

Anyway, as agreed, Allegra wasn't there for my second visit. It was just Mim and me, face to face. From our first conversation, I had salted away the fact that the closest we got to bonding was over the ugliness of certain English words. If any suitable openings arose, verbal was the way to go.

So reconciled was she to my appearance that, when I arrived, she had just pushed down the top of a cafetiere. And the coffee smelt extraordinarily good. Though, when Allegra served it she had used mugs, that day's coffee came in clean, treasured china. In decline she might be, but Mim Galbraith still had style.

Giving me coffee was one thing, but she didn't reckon she knew me well enough to indulge in small talk. I was left in no doubt that I was only present in a professional capacity.

'Now you're here, what do you propose to do?' she asked with some aggression.

'First, clear up the books on the floor, then take down the ones on the shelves, and check how bad the damage is to the shelves themselves.'

'Then tell me which ones you're intending to throw away?' Again, aggressive.

'I won't throw away any books,' I replied evenly, 'other than the ones you ask me to throw away.'

'Oh, you're letting me make the decision?' she asked, with an edge of sarcasm.

'They're your books,' I said.

'I'm glad you recognize that.' She was almost gracious. 'Most of them have sentimental associations, associations with where I bought them or who gave them to me. Though sometimes,' she confessed, 'I actually don't seem able to remember where I bought them or who gave them to me.'

'I'm sure it comes back to you when you look at them closely.'

'Perhaps. Sometimes.' She was lost in a moment of musing. Then she picked up a book from the table beside her chair and said, 'I'm going to read while you get on.'

'That's fine.'

'It's not that I'm keeping an eye on you.'

'It didn't occur to me you might be.'

'No. The other one . . .' She paused. 'The other one didn't like me being in the same room while she was working.'

'Why ever not?'

'She said it made it look as though I didn't trust her.'

'Where you sit is up to you, I'd have thought. It's your house, after all, Miss Galbraith.'

'Not "Miss Galbraith". "Mim".'

Another small breakthrough? 'Very well, Mim,' I said.

'And the other one wanted me to get rid of lots of books.'

'This "other one" you're talking about, Mim,' I asked, 'is she the other decluttering expert Allegra organized for you?'

'Yes. Of course she is. Didn't I say that?'

'No, you didn't. Not in so many words.'

'But you worked out who I was talking about?'

'Yes, Mim.'

'Then there's really no problem, is there?' she said with a slight return of scratchiness.

'No. No problem at all. What was her name, the other declutterer?'

'It was . . . it was . . . Oh, for heaven's sake!' she said angrily. 'It's names, it's always bloody names that get me. I know full well what the name is, but . . .' The look she cast on me was almost paranoid. 'I've forgotten your name now, as well.'

'I'm Ellen.'

'Yes, of course. I knew that!' she snapped.

'And the other declutterer . . .?'

'I don't know. It's gone.'

I didn't want to plant ideas in her head but couldn't stop myself from suggesting gently, 'Was it Rosemary?'

'That's right,' she said. 'Rosemary! Rosemary Findlay was her name.' That was clear enough. My prompt had done the trick. 'Her company had some silly name I can't remember.'

'BrightHome?' I suggested.

'That's right. Bloody stupid name, like I said.'

I was intrigued to know more about my denigrator, my local rival in the decluttering stakes, but I thought I'd better make a start on the books. I didn't want Mim to mark me down as a skiver.

I was determined not to initiate any conversation. I thought it might antagonize her. But if she spoke to me, then of course I would answer.

I had left my toolbox in the Yeti and come in with just soft brushes and dusters. I started by picking up all the books that had fallen on to the floor, wiping them down and piling them up neatly. The ones that had suffered damage, torn pages, broken spines and what-have-you, I put to one side. Nothing was going to get taken out of the house without Mim's express permission. Her strictures about what Rosemary Findlay had done strengthened my resolve, but I would have taken that approach anyway.

Though the content of Mim's library didn't concern me in a professional capacity, my natural curiosity and love of books made me intrigued by what she'd actually collected. And as I might have anticipated, her books offered a comprehensive literary history of the second half of the twentieth century. Many novels whose titles I recognized, with poetry as well represented as fiction.

'Oh, it's so annoying!' she said suddenly.

'What's so annoying?' I asked, looking up from a pile of books.

'I used to know this by heart and, with some of the lines now, it's like I've never seen them before.'

'What are you reading?'

'*Summoned by Bells.*'

'Sorry, I don't know it.'

'Verse autobiography by John Betjeman. Rather good, I think. I know he's often dismissed as being glib and simplistic, but there's a strong undercurrent of emotion, restrained by the rigid verse forms he favoured.'

This was Mim Galbraith in full teacher mode. Precise, definitive. But I didn't think she would have reacted well to pupils who disagreed with her views.

'Did you know Betjeman?' I asked.

'Why should I have done?'

'When we last came to see you, you said you'd met Ted Hughes and Sylvia Plath.'

'Yes, but they were on a very different planet from Betjeman. He was much more of an Establishment figure than Ted.'

'They were both Poet Laureate.'

'Maybe, but they couldn't have come at poetry from more different directions. Ted's writing was instinctive, visceral. Betjeman was much more measured and calculated. As I say, I liked both of their writings, but the two names don't really belong in the same sentence.'

'Oh. Right,' I said, rather feebly. I went back to sorting the books. And Mim went back to *Summoned by Bells*.

There was no further conversation until it was time for me to leave. I had by then checked out her shelves and concluded that their state of dilapidation was beyond my basic DIY skills. I fixed an appointment for the next week and Mim agreed to the idea of Dodge coming with me to assess the job.

When I left, Mim insisted on seeing me to the front door. 'Don't get old, Ellen,' she said, having at least remembered my name. 'It's just not worth the effort.'

My next appointment being in Chichester, I went home for lunch. Assembled scrambled egg with tomato, served on toast (with butter). I'm lucky that I don't have to worry about my weight. Partly, it's metabolic, but also, the amount of lugging furniture and heavy boxes around I do keeps me trim.

The two references I had heard in the past twenty-four hours to Rosemary Findlay intrigued me, so I sought out the BrightHome website. It was professionally done and offered much the same services as SpaceWoman. Like mine, good testimonials from satisfied customers. Though the cynic in me did register how easy it is to fake testimonials. You can put anything you like on a website. No one checks. Mind you, anyone going on to mine might have the same reaction, that they were made up . . . though I hasten to point out that all my accolades are completely genuine.

I found it mildly disturbing how alike the two websites were. Anyone going online, with no prior knowledge or friend's recommendation, could just have tossed a coin for which one to contact.

On BrightHome's there was a photograph of Rosemary Findlay, looking cheering and helpful. But then on SpaceWoman's there's one of me looking equally cheering and helpful.

My rival – whom I was increasingly and unreasonably starting to think of as my enemy – was a woman about my age with blue eyes and blonded hair, worn quite long, bobbing at her shoulders. Carefully chosen make-up – gash of over-red lipstick and those sculpted eyebrows that look as if they've been stuck on. Sorry, I'm not usually as bitchy as this, but something about Rosemary Findlay really annoyed me.

The thought of her website reviews prompted me to have a look on my Facebook page, something I don't do as often as I should. I was much more dependent on it when I founded SpaceWoman. Starting from nowhere, I got a lot of my bookings that way. Now that most come by word-of-mouth personal recommendations, I don't look at Facebook that often. Very rarely anything interesting there. I'm not surprised the younger generation have given up on it.

I hadn't missed much in the way of bookings. Only a couple of enquiries. One who'd made that common old mistake of thinking I did house clearance. And another who, though I'd currently got plenty of work, I would follow up on. When you run your own business, you can't ignore any potential opening.

There was also a new review for SpaceWoman's services. These I rarely check because they're usually from people I've just been working with and . . . I'm afraid I have to say it . . . they are universally grateful and complimentary.

This one, however, wasn't. It read: 'Shoddy job. Ellen Curtis spent far more time chatting than she did decluttering. I would not employ her again and would advise other people not to.'

It felt like a body blow. I wasn't expecting the comments to inflict much reputational damage on SpaceWoman, but they were still unnecessary and hurtful. Hit my pride. Why would anyone be so gratuitously offensive?

The name of the person who had left the review was Edyta Jankowski. Which alone would have told me it was fake. I have never in my life met – let alone worked for – anyone called Edyta Jankowski.

But I had a conviction that the person who had entered the review under Edyta Jankowski's name was Rosemary Findlay. When I take against someone, I take against them.

Roy Waites didn't look anything like Cedric. He must have got his looks from Flick. He was well over six foot and wore his thinning white hair in a pony-tail like some superannuated rock star. Blue jeans and a black leather jacket complemented this image.

His wife Michelle was stocky . . . well, no, fat. Her hair was cropped short and dyed shocking pink. There were studs in the curl of her ears and one perforating the edge of her right nostril. Her leather jacket was brown, above a denim skirt and cowboy boots. The head of a snake tattoo peered out of the top of her shirt.

But, in spite, of their 'statement' appearance, both of them came across as middle-class and rather pernickety. Neither made any secret of the fact that they didn't want to be in Chichester and looked forward to leaving 14 Seacrest Avenue as soon as they possibly could.

'So, you found his body?' said Michelle, as soon as Tim had introduced us.

'Yes.'

If I'd been expecting commiseration for the shock, I was

disappointed. She just asked, brusquely, 'And what were you doing here?'

I explained, as succinctly as I could, about Cedric being hospitalized after his earlier fall, the involvement of the social services, and their employing me to get the old man's life back on track.

'Oh yes,' said Michelle, 'I remember hearing about that fall. Because you were all set to come rushing down here, weren't you, Roy?'

'Well, yes, I did think perhaps—'

'Whereas I knew it was just another of your father's calls for attention. He was always doing things like that.'

She couldn't have made clearer her lack of understanding of and sympathy for her father-in-law. While, at the same time, giving me a neat indication of the balance within her marriage.

I curbed my instinct to defend the late Cedric Waites. I did not want to get involved in the lives of his relations. I had only come to 14 Seacrest Avenue because Tim Goodrich had asked me to. I would answer their questions but, after that, I had already formed the opinion I didn't want to see either Roy or Michelle Waites again. And there was no reason why I ever should.

On seeing Tim Goodrich again I'd reserve judgement.

'So,' Michelle went on, 'since you know the house, maybe you could give us a quote for clearing the place? We want to get it on the market as soon as possible.'

'No, I'm sorry,' I said. 'I don't do house clearance. I do decluttering.'

'Same difference, isn't it?'

Michelle Waites was one of those relatively few people with whom I could quickly lose my temper. Again, I curbed the instinct and said evenly, 'No, you'll get a house clearance company to do it a lot cheaper.'

'Ah.' The appeal to the wallet did seem to carry weight with her.

'But on the other hand,' her husband ventured an opinion, 'if Ellen's on the spot and knows the house, it might make sense for her to do it.'

My instinct to say I didn't want to do the job was another one I curbed. Because in that moment it struck me that, though his son and daughter-in-law appeared to have no interest in Cedric's life, I did. Going through his possessions and papers would be a kind of homage to the old boy.

Also, I couldn't forget Tim's suspicion of 'something funny' about Cedric's death. I was being offered the perfect opportunity to do a little private investigation. I said I'd do the job. Roy was pleased to have one responsibility sorted. Michelle was less keen, until I said I'd knock 10 per cent off my usual decluttering rate. Then she agreed. She was one of those women who needed the satisfaction of having achieved a bargain.

It was agreed that I should hang on to my key and start clearing the house the following morning. Papers and valuables I would put to one side. Things that might have resale potential I should get the best price I could for.

'Don't you want to check through? There might be stuff with sentimental value.'

'Yes,' said Roy. 'There could be stuff of Mum's as well as Dad's. I haven't really got anything to remember her by.'

'No,' said Michelle. 'Just get the best price you can for everything. And chuck the rubbish.' Her husband didn't argue. 'Keep accounts and get invoices. And don't go waltzing off with anything you fancy for yourself.'

So insulted was I by the suggestion that I was momentarily speechless. Fortunately, Tim came to my defence. 'Take that back, Michelle,' he snapped. 'Either you stay down here and check every item Ellen puts up for sale, or you show a bit of trust in a fellow human being. Ellen's been running SpaceWoman for nearly ten years and there has never been a complaint about her honesty.'

I was flattered that he had bothered to remember the name of my company. And embellished it with a bit of positive PR.

Michelle Waites mumbled some graceless apology and then went on the defensive. 'I'm sorry, but this is all stressful for us. Particularly for Roy. He's very mixed up about his reaction to all this, aren't you, love?'

Roy admitted that he was. But he didn't feel he should elaborate. Not when he'd got Michelle there to do it for him.

'It was very difficult for Roy. He thought he had grown up in this perfectly normal family, where his mother and father both loved him. You know, they had disagreements, but that's par for

the course, isn't it? Happens in every family. And when I came
into his life . . . well, they weren't as welcoming as they might
have been. With Roy being an only child, they didn't think any
woman would be good enough for him. They certainly didn't
think I was.'

I could see their point.

'But that settled down. We had disagreements, sure. Like, they
were sorry Roy and I decided it would be irresponsible to have
children . . . you know, given the state of the planet. But, gener-
ally, I'm an accommodating type. I get along with most people.'

Oh yeah? I thought.

'So, we worked out a way of getting along as an extended
family. We didn't see a great deal of each other. Well, we were
all very busy. Cedric and Flick had their work, and you wouldn't
believe how involved in things Roy and are I in Worcester. Then
there's the garden. We're very keen on our garden, aren't we,
Roy?'

'We certainly are,' said Roy enthusiastically. As if he'd dare
to disagree.

'And,' his wife ploughed on, 'when we did get together with
your parents, things were fairly all right. Well, we were all polite
to each other, anyway.

'And then Roy's parents are coming up to retirement, and
soon after that he gets this absolute body blow that his mother's
died. So, we have to come down here for the funeral and
everything.'

She made it sound as if it had been an inconvenient imposition
and went on, 'And I was as helpful to Roy's old man as I could
be over that period, tidying the house, preparing meals for him,
stocking his freezer. I've gone on doing that over the years.
I don't know why I bothered, though. I didn't get any thanks
for it.'

'How long were you down here over the funeral?' asked Tim
Goodrich. I was grateful to him. I wanted to know that too.

'Oh, it had to be three or four days,' said Michelle, again
martyred. Not a vast hole in anyone's schedule, I thought. Not
for a family funeral.

'Then, within six months of that,' she went on, 'we're beginning to think maybe we should make the effort to come down

here and see how the old boy's getting on. So, Roy rings him. It's always Roy who rings. Well, Cedric was his father, not mine. And do you know what Cedric has the nerve to say? He only says, "Don't bother coming down. I don't want to see you." To his own son!'

I wasn't surprised. It's quite a common syndrome, often how the life of a recluse begins. The idea of having someone else in their space becomes gradually less desirable until they can't tolerate the idea. It's relatively easy to put off friends and neighbours. Trickier with family members. And the announcement that the sufferer doesn't want to see a relative can be profoundly destructive. They're almost bound to take it personally, not to realize that it's not just them who the recluse is shutting out of his or her life. It's a blanket ban on everyone from entering the house.

I felt a moment of sympathy for Roy. None for Michelle, though, particularly as she went on, 'So, well, given that response, there's no way we're going to put ourselves out for him, is there? I say that, if Cedric's going to cut himself off from us, then we should cut ourselves off from him. But Roy's more of a sentimentalist than I am. Aren't you, love?'

'I suppose I am, yes,' her husband conceded.

'And dutiful. A dutiful son. Even after that second body blow of being told his father didn't want to see him any more, Roy still rang the selfish old bastard every month. Didn't get a lot of feedback but he kept doing it. He's a very fine man, Roy. What more could he have done?'

I had so many answers to that that, if I hadn't decided to say nothing, I wouldn't have known where to start. Roy Waites, meanwhile, just smiled sheepishly, in acknowledgement of his saintliness.

Michelle looked at her watch. 'We must be off soon. What time are we due at the solicitors?'

'Three o'clock,' Tim replied.

'Good. Then we can get things sorted and finally move on.'

I couldn't believe that 'finally'. Her father-in-law had only been dead a matter of days.

'I wouldn't get too excited, Michelle,' said Tim drily. 'This meeting with the solicitor is just the beginning. Probate can take a very long time to sort out. It'll be a while before you can get this place on the market.'

'I know that,' she said dismissively. 'But at least this afternoon we'll know the exact details of the will. That'll be a start.' She looked sharply at Tim. 'Do you know what's in it?'

He shook his head. 'Cedric didn't tell me.'

'But you're the executor, aren't you?'

'Yes. But there's no law that says the executor has to be told the provisions of the will.'

'Huh. So how long do you reckon we'll be with the solicitor this afternoon?'

'I don't know. An hour?' said Tim.

'Because we don't want to be too late back to Worcester. Early start tomorrow. There's a lot needs doing in the garden.'

'And when will you be coming back here?' he asked.

'What do we have to come back for?'

'Organizing the funeral, for one thing.'

'God,' said Michelle. 'Do we have to do everything?'

I was mildly seething as I unlocked the Yeti outside 14 Seacrest Avenue. Normally I can rationalize why most unpleasant people are unpleasant, and in most cases I end up feeling sorry for them. In Michelle Waites's case, I was prepared to feel straightforward loathing.

'Sorry about that.' I looked up to see that Tim Goodrich had followed me out.

'Oh, don't worry. I meet a varied range of people in my work,' was my tight-lipped response.

He grinned. 'I'd only met Michelle very briefly before. I didn't realize what a complete cow she was.'

That got a grin out of me.

'And good idea of yours, Ellen, to take on the house clearance. I know you don't normally do that kind of stuff. Equally, I know exactly why you're doing it in this case.'

'Might find out something,' I said.

'Yes.'

'Ah.' Over his shoulder, I saw Roy and Michelle coming out of the house. Significantly, she was carrying the closed briefcase that had been under Cedric's bed. At least two grand in twenties.

In the unlikely event of the will not leaving everything to Roy and her, for what she was doing Michelle might be charged with stealing. But I didn't share the thought with the executor.

She gestured impatiently to Tim. 'Come on! We don't want to be late.'

'Coming!' he called across. Then, to me, 'We're walking into the centre. Easier than trying to find somewhere to park there.'

'Very sensible.'

'Listen,' he continued, more quietly, 'I've got to stay down here for a couple of days, see banks and what-have-you – even if the bereaved couple're going straight back to Worcester. Wondered if you might be free for dinner tomorrow night . . .?'

'Might be.'

'If I were to ring you on the number I rang yesterday . . .?'

'That should do it.'

'Tim, are you coming!'

'Yes, Michelle. Talk soon,' he whispered to me.

I wasn't quite as seething as I had been when I left the house.

SIX

I had got into the Yeti and started the engine when I heard a tap on the window. I lowered it and found myself facing a thin, birdlike elderly woman.

'You've just come from Number Fourteen?' she asked.

'That's right.'

'Who was the others? Why was you there, come to that?'

'I'd been helping the owner declutter the place for some months.'

'Oh, you must be that Ellen he talked about.'

'That's right. My name's Ellen Curtis.'

'He had a lot of time for you, Cedric did.'

'I'm glad to hear it. And,' I continued, making a leap of intuition, 'might you be Vi?'

'That's me, right. Who was the others with you in the house?'

'Roy, Cedric's son, and his wife.'

'Oh, so they waited till the old boy was dead to come and see him, did they?'

I didn't comment.

'Who was the other guy then?'

'Tim Goodrich. He's the executor of the estate.'

'Oh, right. Funny, I thought he looked familiar, like I'd seen him round here before.'

'He used to be a GP in Chichester. Maybe you came across him then.'

'I suppose it's possible. Anyway, sorry old Cedric passed.'

I winced inwardly. I'd never liked that expression. So far as I was concerned, however much you sanitized it, death was death and what people did was die. 'Had you known him a long time, Vi?' I asked.

'Since he and Flick moved here. I've lived in the same house in Seacrest Avenue all my life. I was born over there at Number Twenty-Three. So, I've known the Waiteses since they moved in here. Got to be fifty years ago. Before their Roy was born.'

'And back then was Cedric reclusive?'

'How d'ja mean?'

'Was he shy? Did he shut himself off from people, like he had done for the last few years?'

Vi rubbed her chin thoughtfully. 'I'd never really thought about it. I mean, Flick was always the live wire in that couple. She'd do most of the talking . . . but that was all right. That's just how they was in company, Flick chattering away nineteen to the dozen, and Cedric kind of smiling quietly in the background. There was no doubt the marriage worked. They adored each other.'

'So, were you surprised when Cedric cut himself off from everyone after Flick died?'

'Well, it was quite a time before I noticed anything strange. She was the one I'd see more of, you know, out in the streets, round the shops. Took me a while to realize Cedric had cut himself off. I went round to his place . . . I don't know, couple of months after she'd passed. I'd had a flyer through the door about a local art exhibition I thought might interest him. And Cedric wouldn't open the front door to me. Actually talked through the letter-box. Said I'd caught him when he's just got out of the bath and he only had a towel on. But I had my suspicions.

'I went round the next week with another made-up excuse and again he'd only talk to me through the letter-box. He did the bath-towel line again, but I wasn't going to believe that twice, was I? So, I said to him straight, "If you're not going to answer the door to me ever again, you tell me. Then I won't go wasting my time coming round, will I?" And he said it wasn't like that, but I knew it was.'

'How did you know?' I asked.

'I'd had experience of something similar.'

'Oh?'

'My brother Clark, he got that way. Four years older than me he was. Had an apprenticeship, learning to be a garage mechanic, down in Portsmouth. One day he comes home, says he's not going to do it no more. Goes up to his bedroom and doesn't come out of there till he's brought out feet first. Seven years ago it is now that he passed.'

'What,' I asked, 'and the family brought meals to him all that time?'

'Yes. Our mum did and, when she passed, I took over.' She looked at me with a rueful grin. 'It happens surprisingly often, families have someone like Clark at home, someone who never goes out.'

I nodded. I'd come across an unexpected number of such cases.

'Some people,' Vi went on, 'said that that was a waste of a life, his. But it weren't. There was things Clark enjoyed, things that made his life worthwhile. I miss him.

'Anyway . . .' She pulled herself together. 'Because of Clark, I knew what was going on with Cedric. I said, "All right, if that's how you want it to be, I won't bother you no more. But if you want me to do anything, you've got my number. You know, shopping or cooking the odd meal." While Clark was alive, I'd got used to cooking for two every meal. Cedric said thank you, he'd think about it.

'Then, a few months later, he does ring me. He says he's getting most of his food, ready meals and stuff, delivered by . . . Avocado, was it?'

'Ocado.'

'That's right. But he says he wouldn't mind a bit more variety in his diet, so could he take me up on my offer of cooking the odd meal? And I say that's fine and we get into this pattern. Tuesdays and Thursdays I cook an extra portion of what I'm having for my supper and I put it in one of them plastic boxes, Tupperware or something, and I leave them round outside his kitchen door. I don't think he was using the front door by then.

'And Cedric insists on paying me. There's a fiver waiting on the back doorstep every time I get there. And I wasn't doing it for money, but he gets offended if I don't take it, so I do. I never see him, though.

'And first of all, he leaves out the plastic containers, all neatly washed, for me to pick up. And then he starts forgetting to do that . . . or decides he's not going to do it any more . . . I don't know, number of containers went to waste. Not that I mind. I'm happy to do something for the old boy.'

This sounded rich, coming from Vi, who must have been considerably older than Cedric.

'So, when did you last actually see him?'

She drew her breath in as she assessed the question. 'Probably at Flick's funeral, I suppose.'

'And was Roy there?'

'Oh yes. With that pot of poison of a wife.'

'But if you saw them there, I'm surprised you didn't recognize her this afternoon.'

'They wasn't dressed like Hell's Angels at the funeral,' Vi said curtly.

I giggled. 'No. I suppose they wouldn't have been.'

'Nor was she the other time I saw her.'

I should have followed up on that but I was in a hurry. I checked my watch. 'Look, Vi, I've got to be on my way. Could I take your phone number? You know, just in case I need to be in touch over Cedric's things. I'm going to be tidying out the house.'

'Yes, of course.' She gave it to me. Landline beginning with the local code, 01243. I couldn't somehow see Vi having a mobile. Wrong generation. Her surname, it turned out, was Spelling.

I gave her one of the SpaceWoman cards with my contact details. I didn't somehow expect her to be using the email, though.

'I must say,' said Vi as I started the engine, 'I was surprised when I heard that Cedric had passed. I thought he was one of those who would go on for ever.'

Her words, taken together with what Tim had said, made me want to know more about Cedric Waites. I was glad I had taken on the task of sifting through the clues of his life.

I recognized the car that was parked outside my house. Not that I'd seen it that often, but mothers tend to remember surprising details about the women their sons are sleeping with. It was Pippa's.

I found them both in the kitchen making ham and cheese toasties. Now I've tried hard not to be the kind of mother who objects to family members appearing unannounced. So far as I'm concerned, it's Ben's house as much as mine, he can come and go as he likes. But I couldn't suppress a mini-pang at the fact that he'd suddenly turned up without having been in touch at all for the past fortnight.

So, I know it makes me sound like an over-fussy sitcom mother but, given Ben's history, I'm never going to stop worrying about him. Yes, yes, all that two weeks without contacting his old ma probably means is that he's having a very nice time with Pippa, thank you. And if he hadn't turned up as agreed to work on the furniture, Dodge would have told me. So I know he's all right. But all that logic doesn't stop my worst imaginings.

When I entered the kitchen, Pippa threw her arms round me fulsomely. Oh dear, am I being bitchy again to say 'fulsomely'? It's just that I always think there's something theatrical about the intensity of her hugs, as if their vigour is designed to be a measure of their sincerity. The lady protesting too much, perhaps . . .?

Pippa is very pretty. I wouldn't be so churlish as to deny her that. Small, perfectly compact figure, naturally red hair worn very short. 'Elfin' is the adjective that springs to mind. I know mothers shouldn't speculate on the sex lives of their offspring, but I get the feeling she'd be very good in bed. Which is nice for Ben.

And yes, a nurse. Though she wears her caring role lightly. Oops, bitchy again, must stop this.

Once I had been released by Pippa, Ben tapped me lightly on the shoulder and said, 'Hi, Ma.' Always a slight level of irony when he calls me that.

'Hi,' I said. Then, banally, 'All going well?'

'Swimmingly, Ma.' Again, said with irony.

Ridiculously, I couldn't think of what to say next. To my son. To Ben, for God's sake!

'Heard from Jools?' was the best I could come up with.

'No.'

'She seems to have vanished off the radar.'

Ben shrugged. 'She does that from time to time.'

'Yes.'

Awful. I never got becalmed in conversations with Ben. Even when he was in the abyss of one of his depressions, I could always think of something to say to him.

Pippa filled the void. 'Exciting times we live in, eh?'

I was nonplussed. 'Sorry? What are you talking about?'

'Ben's *Riq and Raq* animation has been shortlisted for a TOCA Film Festival Award. Didn't he tell you that?'

'Of course he told me,' I replied, trying not to sound testy. Yes, he'd told me, but I felt marginally miffed that he had told her. I thought we had this principle about keeping the knowledge of shortlisting to the minimum number of people.

I had to face the fact. I was jealous of my son's girlfriend. It wasn't an emotion that I was proud of. 'When are the winners announced?' I asked, though I knew full well.

'Saturday week,' said Pippa.

'I'm trying not to think about it,' said Ben.

'Yes, but you can't stop yourself from thinking about it, can you, Benji?'

No. Not 'Benji'. Please.

'I'm doing my best to.' Then, with a smile to her, 'And I would be succeeding if a certain person didn't keep raising the subject.'

'All right, you can blame me for that,' she said with a winsome little laugh. 'I just know how much difference something like this could make to your career. You're destined for something better than making furniture, Benji. Winning the TOCA could make all the difference. You know that, don't you, Ellen?'

Having had my opinion graciously sought, I dutifully agreed how important winning could be. But I felt uneasy, and I could see that Ben did too. Tempting providence, counting chickens, all that. The kind of thinking that Oliver and I had always avoided.

Then Pippa compounded the offence by saying, 'Benji's *Riq and Raq* animation is bound to win. It's absolutely brilliant! Don't you agree, Ellen?'

And I was put in the humiliating position of admitting that my son hadn't shown the film to me yet.

Ben and Pippa went back to Brighton fairly soon. I never did find out what had brought them to Chichester that day. Still, at least I'd had some contact with my son. I could see that he appeared to be OK. Though I wish I felt more certain that he really was.

That evening I had a call from Tim, confirming dinner the following night, the Tuesday. He'd booked a table for eight o'clock at Purchase's in North Street.

It was a long time since I'd been there. It was a long time since I'd been anywhere like that.

Long time since I'd been on a date. Not, of course, that this was a date.

Dodge was very jumpy on the Tuesday morning as we drove to Mim's in his Commer. He didn't like being driven, would always rather be at the wheel himself. Which was fine by me, the only drawback being that, because we were travelling in the van, I had to transfer some of my basic equipment from the back of the Yeti.

Dodge is naturally taciturn and I'm used to doing most of the talking when we're together. But I've never known him as clammed up as he was that morning.

He only broke his silence once. I was talking about the set-up at 14 Seacrest Avenue and how I'd agreed to take on the clearance of the premises. (I didn't mention that I was having dinner with the estate's executor that evening.) I was idly speculating about the cause of Cedric's death, when Dodge said suddenly, 'I can't get over the fact that I was the last person to see him alive. I should have checked on him more carefully. Maybe there was something I could have done.'

Dodge was equally silent when we got to Mim's, but that was not unusual. He was always shy around people, particularly new people. It had taken me a long time to establish a relatively chatty relationship with him (the relationship of which there was no evidence that morning).

But it was fine. A part of Mim Galbraith's rather grand manner seemed to involve ignoring tradespeople, so she made no overtures to Dodge. It made me feel fortunate to have been acknowledged and even offered coffee on my introduction to her. But maybe that was because I had the validation of being brought into the house by Allegra. Although I was there in a professional capacity, her introduction had made my visit more of a social event.

I wasn't offered coffee that morning. Nor was Dodge. He would have said no, anyway. His tipple of choice is nettle tea.

So, while he got on with measuring the shelves that would need replacing, I sat and chatted with Mim. In anticipation of

seeing her, I had the previous evening dug out my tattered paperback of Sylvia Plath's *Colossus, and Other Poems*. It brought
back recollections of teenage angst.

'I had a look at "Spinster",' I said to Mim.

'What?'

'"Spinster", the Sylvia Plath you mentioned when I first met
you.'

'I know, I know,' she said testily.

'It reminded me how much I liked it. The woman in the poem
has power, she builds up her defences against men.'

'Yes. That's the kind of thing feminist critics seize upon with
Sylvia.' Mim was back in confident, schoolteacher mode. 'I'm
not sure that she really was that much of a feminist, certainly
not when I knew them. The brightness of that particular aura has
been added by the Plath myth-builders.'

'Probably,' I said, well aware that this was a subject on which
I knew considerably less than she did.

'And there is certainly no lack of that cohort,' pronounced
Mim without full approval. 'Hordes of minor academics have
jumped on the Ted-bashing bandwagon. Particularly bloody
Americans. American academics seem to have far too much
time to take up causes. But, of course, they didn't know them
as I did.'

'This was when Ted and Sylvia lived in London?'

'Yes. I'd known him first at Cambridge. Then, later, he and
Sylvia lived in Primrose Hill. Fitzroy . . . Fitzroy . . . I can't
remember whether it was "Road" or "Avenue". Or what number
theirs was. Twenty . . . twenty something? Oh, I used to know
this!' The last sentence was almost petulant with frustration.

I thought a change of subject might save her further pain.
'When I was here with Allegra, you mentioned that she'd
organized another declutterer for you.'

'Yes. What of it?'

'And apparently that hadn't worked out. You said they didn't
like books.'

'They didn't. They just wanted me to get rid of books. They
didn't seem to realize that books are the continuity of my life. I
didn't have children. The right time and the right man never coincided. And yes, there were my pupils, whose company I enjoyed

while they were under my tutelage. But I didn't stay in touch with them. I always had a new intake to get to know, and they had their own lives to lead, mostly lives on the treadmill of marriage and children. But my books reflect different times for me. Different friends, different lovers . . . They are the . . . As I say, the . . .'

At the end of the long, articulate speech, the memory let her down again. '"The continuity of your life",' I suggested gently.

'Yes,' she snapped. 'I was about to say that.'

'And we established that this other declutterer was called Rosemary Findlay.'

'What of it?'

'I just wondered, when you said "things didn't work out", whether you'd actually had a row, or how the business relationship ended.'

'I found her putting books into cardboard boxes to take away. And she hadn't checked with me which books I wanted to part with. She seemed to feel her job was just to make space in the house by clearing everything out. I wasn't going to tolerate that. She treated me as if I was some kind of imbecile, incapable of making up her own mind about anything.'

'Ah. Well, I promise you I won't get rid of anything you don't want got rid of.'

'Good. You ask how my "business relationship" with the Findlay woman ended.' Mim had good recall of certain details. 'I told her that if she didn't have more respect for people's property, then she was in the wrong line of work. And then she had the nerve to send me an invoice for the hours she had done.'

'Did you pay it?'

'Yes. A small price to get her definitively out of my life.'

Things Mim had said about her past intrigued me and I took advantage of her current lucidity to ask, 'You said you knew Ted Hughes at Cambridge?'

'Yes, I was a sort of hanger-on with the lot he went around with. Lucky to be included, they really thought I was too posh. But I was sleeping with one of them, so they tolerated me for his sake. A lot of drinking cider at The Mill pub and singing folk songs, I recall. Not really my social scene but back then, as a woman, your interests had to reflect those of the man you were with.'

'And you said you saw Ted Hughes in London when he was married to Sylvia Plath?'

'Yes, a bit. I was sleeping with another of their friends by then, well, someone in their circle. There were other poets they saw a great deal of then. Like Peter . . . Peter . . .? Oh, damn, I can see his face. What was his bloody name? Peter . . .?'

But the clouds of forgetfulness had closed over again.

In the Commer driving back to Chichester, Dodge did not initiate any conversation. At one point, I asked him if he was going to use wood from pallets (his favourite building material) to replace the broken shelves in Mim's house.

'No,' he said, 'Not strong enough, for one thing. And won't match the originals. I've got a load of wood planks saved from a school they were demolishing. It's the right quality and I can stain it to match.'

I should have known. The unoccupied house that Dodge owned was stacked to the rafters with all kinds of salvage. He had the right wood there for any repair job.

'And the furniture you're making with Ben – that all going well?'

He didn't answer. He didn't say another word till he was about to deposit me outside my house, where the Yeti was parked. Then he answered my question.

Dodge was such an anomaly but, through the layers of trauma, his ingrained middle-class good manners usually asserted themselves. 'About the furniture,' he said awkwardly, his gaze as ever averted from me, 'it's busy. There's a playschool in Littlehampton got flooded when a water main burst. All the desks were ruined. I'm replacing them. Got to get a move on.'

He said no more, no goodbye, just drove off.

Oh dear, I thought, that's going to be another job he'll be doing for free. Which will lead to more unspoken friction with Ben. Their working relationship just wasn't going to last.

I found myself praying to the God I didn't believe in that my son's *Riq and Raq* animation would win the TOCA Award. With all the positive career boosts that might follow.

I was determined not to take more trouble than usual with dressing for my dinner at Purchase's. It wasn't a date, after all.

I went for dark navy trousers and a plain shirt with a mandarin collar. Grey . . . well, Moon Grey I'm pretty sure it was called. And, with the evenings getting warmer, all I needed on top was a cardigan in Soft White. All Eileen Fisher. Good quality, not ostentatious. And a very long time since I'd worn them.

While I was checking out my make-up in the mirror, my SpaceWoman mobile rang. It was after six and, since I try to separate work and life (though they spill over into each other all the time), I let it go to message.

When I checked, it was a Gerry Cullingford who'd called. There couldn't be many people with that name around. Must be the husband of Lita. He asked me to ring him back. What on earth could he want? I'd call him in the morning.

A final check in the mirror convinced me that I wasn't wearing enough colour. I changed the Moon Grey shirt for a jersey top in Papaya.

Not that it mattered. After all, it wasn't a date.

SEVEN

'I still don't know the terms of Cedric's will,' said Tim.

We had just ordered. I'd gone for the Roasted Partridge Breast starter, followed by the Pan-Fried Fillet of Salmon. I don't believe in that stuff about only white wine with fish and said I'd rather drink red, 'a Merlot or something'. Tim upgraded to an Argentinian Malbec which, when it arrived, was extremely good.

'Really? Isn't that odd, if you're the executor?' I asked.

'Not that odd. As I explained before, I just agreed to be his executor as a favour and never expected to have to take on the job myself. I assumed he'd predecease Flick and she'd sort out the estate. I also assumed that everything would be left to Roy – or Roy and Michelle.'

He paused. 'Are you saying,' I asked, 'that that is not the case?'

'No. As I say I have, as yet, no knowledge of the will's contents,' said Tim with a grin. 'But I'd be interested to see Michelle's reaction if everything wasn't left to them. You may have noticed her lording it around the place when we were at Seacrest Avenue.'

'Yes, I did.' I was tempted to mention the fact that she'd swanned off with over two thousand quid in Cedric's briefcase, but didn't think it was the moment. 'So, there was no dramatic "Reading of the Will Scene", so beloved of melodramatic screenwriters, when you went to the solicitors yesterday?'

'No. That can't really happen properly until a Grant of Probate has been made. I'm afraid the meeting was a bit of a damp squib, really. All that was agreed was that, when we needed the help of a solicitor in sorting out the estate, they were the solicitors we would instruct. Though I'm not actually sure why. I wasn't impressed by their efficiency. Although it was with them that Cedric and Flick had drawn up their will, they couldn't immediately put their hands on a copy of it. Came up with a feeble excuse about having recently moved offices. But they promised they'd find it within twenty-four hours.'

'So, have you had another meeting with them today? Did Roy and Michelle stay over?'

'No. They didn't change their plan. Went back to Worcester yesterday afternoon, as originally intended. Their garden called to them. Actually, they left in high dudgeon. I arranged to pick up a copy of the will this afternoon, because I was staying down here . . .' he grinned '. . . not least because I had a rather attractive dinner date set up for this evening.'

It was a potentially cheesy line but Tim's ironic tone stopped it from being cheesy.

'So, presumably you've read the will?'

'No, I haven't. That's what's so frustrating. The bloody solicitors still haven't found it. Well, they swear they now know where it is and I can get it tomorrow morning. Which is annoying because it means I'll lose another full day's work. I'd been intending to start back for Oxford first thing.'

At that moment our starters arrived. Before I embarked on my Roasted Partridge Breast, I said, 'And when you have seen the will? As an executor, are you not allowed to tell other people its contents?'

'"Other people" being you, perhaps?'

'Well, all right, yes.' He grinned sardonically. 'Sorry, Tim, it's just that I got so caught up in Cedric's life in his last months. And I am a naturally curious person.'

'Are you?' he teased.

'Yes. But I'm fully prepared to accept that it's not my business.'

'In spite of the fact that you're desperate to know?'

'You sum up my position very accurately.'

Tim took a teasing mouthful of his Goat's Cheese & Basil Mousse before saying, 'I don't think there's anything in the rules of being an executor which prohibits me from discussing the contents of the will with anyone I choose to discuss them with. So, I'll be happy to let you know the will's contents, though probably not before I've given the information to the people who might be most closely involved.'

'You mean Roy and Michelle?'

'I do.' He took another pause and another mouthful of mousse. He was enjoying his control of the narrative. But then he seemed to lose his nerve. 'Maybe I shouldn't talk about it, though,' he said.

'What?'

'Sorry. Thinking about my role as executor, I don't think I should really be talking about the details of the will to anyone until we've got the Grant of Probate.'

'If you think that's the right thing to do.'

'I do, I'm afraid. Sorry. I'll tell you the details as soon as Roy and Michelle know.'

Which, I suppose, was fair enough.

Fortunately, once the conversation moved away from the affairs of the Waites family, the evening got much more relaxed.

And enjoyable.

We talked more, talked very easily, about ourselves. A bit of background. I told Tim I was a widow but didn't go into details of how Oliver died. Time enough for that when we'd spent more time together. If, of course, we did spend more time together.

And Tim told me a bit about his past. There had to be one. No man as attractive as him was going to get to his fifties without some kind of emotional backstory.

As I'd rather suspected, the move from being a GP in Chichester to being a research scientist in Oxford had coincided with a change in his domestic circumstances. A divorce, inevitably perhaps. The only detail he supplied was that it had saddened him. No mention of his ex-wife's name and the strong suggestion that they'd seen nothing of each other since the official ending of the marriage. But I think most men say that about their ex-lovers when they meet someone new.

Not, of course, that I was 'someone new' in Tim's life. Not in that sense.

The meal was good, the conversation – as I said – easy, and the Malbec did its stuff. When we left Purchase's, we both felt very mellow.

Tim was staying at the Chichester Harbour Hotel, the other side of the road from Purchase's. He offered to walk me home, but it wasn't fully dark and I was used to being around Chichester on my own. Also, I didn't relish the prospect of awkwardness on my doorstep.

He was going back to Oxford the next morning. He said he'd inevitably have to be back at some point to deal with the legal stuff. And he'd be in touch with me about the clearance of 14 Seacrest Avenue.

So, with the gentlest of pecks on my cheek, Tim Goodrich went his way. And I went mine.

I felt good. It does a girl good to be pampered occasionally.

And it was a very long time since this particular girl had been pampered.

When I got home, there were a couple of messages on my landline answering machine.

The first one was from Fleur, asking if I could join her for lunch the next day at the spa attached to the Goodwood Hotel. It's her place, where an extremely minimal workout in variegated Lycra, to her mind, justifies a very boozy lunch. She knows I can rarely go midweek, because I am actually running a business called SpaceWoman. Which, she knows full well, is not a cleaning service.

As an appeal to my guilt, in her message Fleur adds that she wants to talk about Jools. She's worried that it's been so long since she heard from her favourite – and indeed only – granddaughter.

I will call her in the morning to say I'm not free for lunch.

The second message was from a Detective Inspector Bayles. He would be grateful if I could give him a call on the Wednesday morning.

He didn't say what it was about.

I'm a businesswoman, so I did my SpaceWoman calls before I got back to the police.

I rang Gerry Cullingford's number and he confirmed that he was Lita's husband. I asked if he was missing his golf clubs and he said no. He didn't enquire what I had done with them and cut me off when I started to tell him about Grant's charity initiative.

'I wonder if you could come to the house again, Ellen.'

'Well, I could, but what for?'

'It's a surprise I want to organize for Lita. For our wedding anniversary.'

'Oh? You do know that what I do is decluttering.'

'Yes, I'm fully aware of that. There's something I've been promising to get cleared out for Lita for a long time.'

'A clearance firm could do that.'

'No, no, the stuff needs sorting. A lot of it could be recycled.'

The appeal to my principles – not to mention a degree of curiosity – persuaded me. I suggested I should go back to Halnaker the next day. No, Gerry wouldn't be there then and Lita would. Then he was away on business. Have to be the following week. The Wednesday worked for both of us. We fixed a time. Two thirty in the afternoon.

I would ring Fleur later to say I couldn't do lunch. Later, while she was actually in the Goodwood gym doing her leisurely work-out. With a mother like mine, you get very good at knowing the times when she won't be able to get to the phone and you can safely just leave a message.

I rang Detective Inspector Bayles.

He could only be described as 'jolly'. Or perhaps 'avuncular'. A large man in brown corduroy trousers. A dark grey zip-up fleece open to show a beer belly straining against a distended tattersall check shirt. Tousled hair, ginger fading to auburn. His image was more of a friendly publican than a policeman.

He arrived at my house on his own, which suggested to me that his inquiries would be relatively casual. My viewing of television police dramas implied that for more important evidence-gathering excursions, they worked in pairs. (Or maybe it was just that two of them could use dialogue to explain the plot to each other and, conveniently, to the viewers at the same time.)

Bayles accepted my offer of tea and casually joined me in the kitchen while I made it. He talked local things, like the increasing problem of parking in central Chichester. Chatty, relaxed. But when he was sitting down with his cup in my sitting room, his manner became more focused.

'What the general public don't seem to realize about police work is that we often start on an investigation with absolutely no information. OK, sometimes we're dealing with known criminals, guys who've been on our radar for years, but in most cases we have nothing more than a name on the electoral register. We don't know the financial circumstances of the characters involved, their family set-up, nothing.

'So, we begin by making a list of people who might have had recent dealings with the deceased and asking them questions. And, because we're starting from nothing, we have to ask some very basic questions, which sometimes have the unfortunate effect of making us sound stupid.' He grinned. 'The image of the police in fiction rarely projects us as the sharpest knives in the drawer, does it?'

'Not very often,' I agreed. 'Certainly not in Golden Age whodunits.'

'No. That Agatha Christie has a lot to answer for.' He grinned again. I wondered whether he talked crime fiction with all his interviewees, of whether he'd intuitively found the right level for conversation with me.

'So,' he went on, 'I really know nothing about Cedric Waites. The first time I heard the name was when I got news of his death. Ellen, perhaps you could explain to me how you came to be involved in his life?'

I did as he asked. He instantly got the differences between decluttering, house clearing and cleaning. Behind his easy manner there was a sharp intellect.

'And you get the impression that Cedric Waites shut himself off from all company from the time of his wife's death?'

'I think it was probably a gradual process over a few months, but yes, her death seems to have been the trigger.'

'And is that common in the . . . er, decluttering world?'

'Not uncommon. Bereavement can lead to strange behaviours.'

'Right. So not only did Cedric Waites not go out, he also wouldn't let anyone from outside into his house?'

'That seems to have been the case, yes.'

'But he made an exception for you?'

'It took a while, but yes, he did eventually let me into the house. He didn't actually have a lot of choice in the matter. If he hadn't let me in, he would have been rehoused by the social services.'

'Mm.' The detective inspector ran his hands ruminatively over his substantial stomach. 'And then, I gather, once he'd allowed you in, he also let in workmen to sort out his central heating and other stuff that needed doing?'

'Yes.'

'Maybe I'll need to talk to them as well as you.'

'I can give you their contacts if you need them.'

'Thank you.' But there didn't seem to be any urgency about the follow-up. 'I was just thinking . . . it must've been difficult for the old boy to organize food deliveries . . . if he never went out and he wouldn't let anyone else in.'

'He seemed to have got that sorted. Deliveries from Ocado, paid for online. A few friends and neighbours might sometimes cook for him, leave little containers of food by his back door.'

'And he'd keep those in the freezer to eat as and when he needed something?'

'That seemed to be the way it worked, yes. The freezer was pretty disgusting, but he must've known how to defrost it. If he hadn't done that from time to time, it would have seized up completely, like his central heating boiler.'

'Hm. So . . . do you know if Cedric Waites kept a close watch on the use-by dates on the stuff in his freezer?'

'I don't actually know, but I would have thought it was unlikely.'

'Not a very healthy lifestyle then?'

'No.'

'Did you ever cook for him, Ellen?'

'Once or twice, when we were first getting to know each other . . . you know, if I'd over-catered. Say I'd expected my son to be home for a meal and then he wasn't.' There had been an increasing number of occasions like that since Ben had got together with Pippa. 'So, I'd popped the extra into a container for Cedric and he'd put it in the freezer and, I don't know, ate it at some point.'

'And do you know how Cedric Waites disposed of the containers his food had been in?'

'That was an issue when I first came to the house.' I told the detective inspector how much time I'd spent clearing the debris of containers in the early days.

'And what did you do with them?'

'I took them to the dump. Most were recyclable.'

'Right.' Another thoughtful, double-handed stroke of the stomach. 'You may be wondering, Ellen, why I'm so interested in the dead man's food containers.'

'I'm sure you'll tell me in time.'

'Hm. Yes. Yes, I will.' He luxuriated in a long pause. 'The fact is, Ellen, because he hadn't seen a doctor recently, an autopsy was performed on Cedric Waites's body.'

'I'd assumed there would be one. It was done quite quickly.'

'Yes. Very efficient they are down there, doing . . . what they do.' Another pause. 'What the autopsy revealed was that what killed him was poison.'

'Oh? What poison?'

'Hasn't been confirmed yet. There are a few possibilities. They're doing further tests.'

'Well . . .'

The detective inspector looked straight at me. 'You don't seem very surprised, Ellen.'

'No. I'm saddened, obviously. But the way Cedric shovelled everything into that freezer . . . let's say it didn't meet the highest health-and-safety standards. And, as we were discussing, I don't think he was very systematic about use-by dates. So, for him to have eaten something that was off . . . well, the surprise really is that it hadn't happened earlier.'

'Hm. Yes. Well, that's a point of view . . . if, of course, the poisoning was accidental.'

'What? You're not suggesting—?'

'We'll know when the test results come back. Since we got the result of the autopsy, we have inspected the premises where Cedric Waites lived. No evidence of any food containers for the last meals he ate.'

'No. I took them.'

'Did you, Ellen? Why would you do that?'

'Well . . . It's what I'd done with the previous ones and, in my line of business, you develop an instinct for tidying things up.'

'I'm sure you do, Ellen. So, where are the containers now? In your bin here?'

'No. I took them to the dump.'

'Did you?'

'Yes. Only on Monday. Surely, if you needed to check them out, it would be easy to retrieve them from . . .'

My words dried up as Bayles slowly shook his head. 'Yes, they do that all the time on television shows, don't they, go through all the jettisoned rubbish? And then they find the vital piece of evidence just before the commercial break. Have you any idea what mounting a search like that through a huge municipal dump . . . any idea what that costs?' He shook his head ruefully. 'No, our budgets are stretched tight enough as it is.'

He looked straight at me again. His expression was hard to read.

'What are you saying, Inspector?'

'I'm just saying that to an outside observer . . . like, to take a random example, me . . . taking those food containers to the dump so quickly . . . looks like rather unusual behaviour.'

There was no doubt about the nature of his expression now. It was one of suspicion.

EIGHT

My interview with Detective Inspector Bayles had left me mildly rattled. I wouldn't put it stronger than that. My conscience was clear and I knew that further investigation would very quickly get me off the hook. I did feel bloody stupid, though, for having chucked out the food containers. Never touch anything at a crime scene – God, how many times have I heard that in police series? Except, of course, at the time I didn't know I was at a crime scene.

So, yes, I felt stupid. Guilty? Not a bit.

But my curiosity had been piqued and – since I didn't have any other SpaceWoman appointments booked for that day – I went straight round to 14 Seacrest Avenue for what Roy and Michelle Waites thought of as a clearance job and I was thinking of increasingly as an investigation. I had assembled myself a hasty cheese sandwich which I ate in the car.

As I approached the house, the possibility occurred to me that it might be sealed off with police tape. But no. Maybe because they were only regarding it as a possible scene of crime, they hadn't gone to those lengths. I felt quite reassured by that.

My key still let me in through the kitchen door. I was just planning my clearance campaign when the mobile rang.

Oh dear. Fleur. And Fleur in full martyr mode.

'I suppose I have to blame myself, don't I, Ellen? They always say blame the parents for their children's shortcomings, particularly when it comes to plain old-fashioned things like bad manners.'

'What have I done to offend you now?' I asked drily.

'I was always taught – and I hope I had taught you too, though clearly I failed there – that it was common politeness to answer invitations.'

I got it. 'I'm sorry. I was going to ring you. Something came up.'

'Oh yes. There's always "something", isn't there? Something

more important than your mother, anyway. So here am I sitting in the Bar and Grill at Goodwood and they're asking me if I want a table for one or two, and I can't tell them because my daughter hasn't had the basic good manners to reply to my invitation.'

I was tempted to tell her that the 'something' that had turned up hadn't been trivial. It had been an interview with the police. But no, that would raise more questions than it avoided.

I was about to apologize again but Fleur got in ahead of me. 'So, what shall I tell them? Is it a table for one or for two? Is my daughter going to deign to join me for lunch?'

'Fleur, you know full well that I'm very rarely free for lunch on a weekday. I do have a business to run.'

'Oh, surely you can get another cleaner to step in every now and then?'

I ought to be immune by now to that little tug of annoyance that the 'cleaner' jibe always gave me. But at least I'm canny enough never to rise to it.

'Fleur, I can't. And I'm just starting on a new job now, so I'm going to have to ring off. Maybe we could get together some time over the weekend . . .?'

'I don't know what I'll be doing at the weekend. I don't know what Kenneth'll be doing at the weekend.'

He'll be playing golf, like he does every other bloody weekend. But I didn't say it.

'I really do need to talk to you soon, Ellen. I'm very worried about what's happening with Jools. It's weeks now since I heard from her. And, although you don't seem to show much interest in what happens to your daughter, I do very much care what happens to my granddaughter.'

Once I'd finally finished the phone call, I decided I'd make a start emptying the cupboards in Cedric's kitchen. But, annoyingly, Fleur's words had got to me. And I started worrying about what might have happened to Jools.

When it happens, a suicide can be quite low key, making the small, sad splash of a stone slipped into a pond. But, from the way the ripples from the impact spread over time, it might as well have been a bloody great boulder.

Nearly ten years on, I'm still feeling the shock of Oliver's death. I'm sure it exacerbated the problems Ben has had with his mental health. But it's a subject that rarely comes up with Jools.

Hardly surprising, because I don't have that many conversations with my daughter. We did touch on it when Jools and I had an uncharacteristic moment of rapprochement in her Herne Hill flat. I had ended up spending the night there a year or so back, while I was following enquiries into the death of the war reporter Ingrid Richards. And just for a moment, Jools talked about her father's death.

That was unusual, though. A momentary chink in the carapace she has built over herself, and quickly sealed up again. The one thing that I recalled her saying was that not talking about Oliver was her way of coping with his death.

Her way of coping with other aspects of her life seems very efficient. She organized the flat purchase herself. I helped her out with the deposit, which she is paying back regularly, according to the schedule we agreed. And Jools seems to be managing her career very well. She's in the world of fashion, though precisely what she does there is a little obscure to me.

It's fashion journalism, so far as I can gather. But no printed magazines involved, it's all online. And it's very much the cheap disposable end of the market. Whether my daughter chose that area deliberately to antagonize me, I don't know. To be fair to her, I think it's unlikely. But she cannot have been unaware of my aims to reuse or recycle anything that can be reused or recycled.

I made one slightly unnerving discovery when I stayed in Herne Hill. After Jools had left in the morning (just leaving a goodbye note for me), I had a look . . . No, I'd better be honest about it, I snooped in her spare room.

I found no bed in there. It couldn't be used for guests. Instead, it was full of racks on which were hung a huge variety of brand-new garments. Exotic and disposable, the kind that were designed only to be worn a few times and chucked out. The kind, all too many of which end up in landfill.

I never asked Jools for an explanation, partly because that would have entailed my owning up to the snooping.

But it did strike a warning note. Through my work, I've encountered many different kinds of hoarding behaviour. And, though I'm not suggesting Jools belonged in that category, it did suggest to me that my daughter's character might not be as straightforward as she wanted it to appear. Surely nobody could be that unaffected by losing a father in the circumstances that she did?

I was mulling over these thoughts, while mechanically removing long-out-of-date cereal packets from Cedric's kitchen cupboards, when my mobile rang. It was Ben.

'Hi, Ma,' he greeted me with his customary irony.

'Hi. All well?' Sorry, it's knee-jerk. Ninety-nine per cent of the times Ben rings me, there is no problem. It's the one per cent that are always with me, though.

'Fine, fine, fine. Pippa sends her love.' I'm afraid my first, unworthy thought was: Trying the charm offensive, is she?

'I just wondered,' Ben went on, 'if you knew where Dodge might be?'

'Where're you calling from?'

'The workshop? I've got my own keys. No sign of him. The Commer's not here either.'

'Had you fixed to meet up today?'

'Yes. We've got a rush job on.'

'Is that making the new desks for the playschool that got flooded?'

'Excellent, Ma. You are well informed.'

'Dodge told me when I last saw him.'

'Which was . . .?'

'Yesterday. He was measuring up some shelves for a client I've got over Midhurst way. And he told me then there was time pressure for the playschool job.'

'Mm. Yes. I suppose it was yesterday when I last spoke to him. He was very insistent I should be here today.'

'He's probably gone off to source some materials he needs for the desks,' I suggested.

'Yes.' Ben didn't sound convinced. I wasn't either, come to that.

'I'd better get on,' he said. 'And thank you, Ma.'

'For what?'

'Not mentioning the bloody TOCA Award thing.'

'Ah.' I didn't want to sound critical, but . . . 'Does that imply you're hearing a lot about it from Pippa?'

'And how! I mean, it's lovely having a girlfriend who's so supportive and backing me all the way and is there for me and . . . but with something like this I just want to forget about it.'

'Not tempt providence?'

'You have it in one, Ma. But Pippa just won't keep quiet about it. Her imagination's running riot. Has no doubt I'm going to win, and then the TOCA Award will lead to other things. I think, in her mind's eye, she's already planning the dress she'll wear when she joins me on the red carpet at the Oscars.'

'She's proud of you, Ben.'

'I guess.'

'I'm very proud of you, too.'

'Yes, but you don't go on about it all the time.'

'I try not to,' I said, trying to suppress the gleeful feeling that I'd somehow got one over on Pippa. I'd certainly never before heard my son express anything that could be construed as criticism of her.

God, what an unpleasant woman I am! I hope I'm not going to become more jealous and embittered as I get older. Why am I so anti-Pippa? Would I be equally antagonistic to any woman who got her claws into my precious son? No, I really took to Tracey, Ben's former girlfriend, on the brief occasion I met her.

Hm. I suppose I'm not the first mother not to have approved her son's choice of partner. There must be some basis of fact behind all those mother-in-law jokes. It does make me feel horribly mean-spirited, though.

My son and I ended the conversation. I didn't tempt providence by wishing him luck for the TOCA verdict in ten days' time. I knew Ben appreciated that.

It took me a while to get back to my clearing of Cedric's possessions. I had someone new to worry about.

When Detective Inspector Bayles had suggested getting in touch with the men who'd worked at 14 Seacrest Avenue, I'd had a flicker of anxiety. No problem with Dean the central heating engineer. But Dodge . . .

Dodge and the police just don't fit in the same sentence. I

don't know the precise details but it was something to do with the major breakdown which converted Gervaise the City slicker into Dodge the silent recycler. I think drugs were involved at some level and maybe it's a criminal record that makes him so wary round the Boys in Blue. He certainly doesn't want to have anything to do with them.

And my basic fear was that a telephone call from Detective Inspector Bayles asking to meet might have made Dodge do a runner.

There wasn't that much more to do in the kitchen. I put the contents of the drawers in boxes. Nothing of value. Ordinary cutlery has virtually no resale potential. That's why you see so much of it at car boot sales. Hallmarked silver would be worth selling, but there was none of that at 14 Seacrest Avenue. However, I knew local charities which would be very grateful for basic kitchenware in the hostels they ran. Michelle Waites had told me to 'chuck the rubbish'. If I could chuck it where it might help someone, all to the good.

Finishing off the basic tidying of the kitchen was a job I'd done so many times I was on automatic pilot. Which was a pity because it didn't distract me from the worries churning in my mind. Worries about Dodge. Worries about Jools. And the permanent background worry about Ben.

Things got better, however, when I moved into the sitting room. I had been in there a few times, but most of my meetings with Cedric had been in the kitchen. Initially to discuss the various tasks that needed to be done around the house and, latterly, for cups of tea and chats.

I had noticed that there were a good few books on the sitting-room shelves but hadn't had the opportunity to look at them closely. Now that I did, I found treasures much more efficient at distracting my mind than kitchenware.

One thing I have observed from my dealings with hoarders is that most of them have some area of tidiness in their lives. They may seem unaware that their clutter has rendered their rooms impassable but there'll be a small oasis of order in the chaos. I had one client who, though her bedroom floor was a foot high with discarded garments, kept the contents of her knicker and

bra drawers in perfectly folded neatness. Or another, the route
to whose attic was an obstacle course of domestic detritus but
whose model railway layout up there was a picture of cleanliness,
where the trains ran on time.

And, though, compared to some of my more deranged clients,
Cedric Waites was well up the tidy end of the hoarding spectrum,
the precision with which his books were arranged suggested that
this was where his true obsession lay. It also perhaps gave an
answer to the question which had niggled away at me since he'd
first come into my life. How, alone in a house with no working
radio or television, did Cedric fill his days?

He didn't have books on the scale that Mim Galbraith did, but
the ones he had were in a much better state of preservation. On
one sitting-room wall were two sets of purpose-built shelves with,
between them, a glass-fronted bookcase. A cursory examination
made it clear that therein were his real treasures.

I like books but I make no claims to know much about them,
certainly not to be an expert collector. All I ask for is something
that's in a readable font, with a jacket that isn't too ugly and –
most important of all – a story that really grabs me. Almost all
I read is fiction, except for work-related stuff, studies of hoarding
case histories, advances in cognitive behavioural therapy tech-
niques, that kind of thing. And, like most people, I regret I don't
devote as much time to reading as I would like to. When you're
tired, the television's always the easier and lazier option.

I wouldn't say, like Mim, that books had been the continuity
of my life but, in some cases, I can remember exactly where I
bought or read something. There are also books I go back to
when I'm stressed or exhausted. If I'm really emotionally
depleted, Dodie Smith's *I Capture the Castle* can usually get me
back on an even keel.

Cedric, though, was clearly more serious about his books. In
my previous brief visits to his sitting room, I hadn't noticed, but
the shelves and the bookcase had undergone a much more
assiduous cleaning regime than the rest of the house. Five days
after their owner's demise, there still wasn't a speck of dust on
them, When I opened the glass doors of the bookcase, the state
of its contents suggested that each book had been recently
removed and lovingly dusted down.

There was a pattern to Cedric's collection. Mostly fiction of the first half of the twentieth century. Names like G.K. Chesterton, Anthony Hope, Graham Greene, George Orwell, Evelyn Waugh. And, looking at them, I saw they were all, if not actually first editions, valuable ones. Inside each, along with the bookseller's description, the purchase paperwork had been punctiliously kept. Most had been bought through a bookseller called Augustus Mintzen. And I was amazed by the prices.

This clearly raised a new dilemma. Michelle Waites's casual 'Just get the best price you can for everything' didn't anticipate there being anything of much value in the house. Cedric's book collection changed the dynamics. I didn't want to put myself at risk of being accused of selling off his precious volumes cheaply. In SpaceWoman I have to be extra cautious about where I dispose of stuff, particularly after a death. Bereavement can bring out the best in some people; it can make others nakedly acquisitive.

Someone like me can get caught in the crossfire of all kinds of accusations: that I've thrown away stuff people wanted to keep, that I've kept stuff that they wanted to get rid of. And, since television antiques programmes have made everyone think they're an expert in valuation, I'm often criticized for not getting nearly enough cash for items I've been asked to sell. I've even on occasion been taken to task for stealing the possessions of the deceased.

All of these experiences have made me very circumspect about jobs like the clearance of 14 Seacrest Avenue.

'Hello?' He sounded cautious on the phone.

'It's Ellen Curtis.'

'Who?' Clearly my name hadn't registered on our recent encounter.

'Ellen from SpaceWoman. You and your wife asked me to clear out your father's house.'

'Oh yes. How can I help you? Sorry, it'll have to be quick. I have to give a lecture in ten minutes.'

'A lecture? In what?'

'Comparative Religion. Michelle and I are both academics.'

'Ah.'

'Her specialty's Women's Studies.'

Why did that not surprise me? 'Look, I'm just wondering what you want me to do about your father's collection of books.'

'I didn't know he had a collection of books.'

'Yes. A lot of twentieth-century fiction. Some first editions. Hadn't he always had an interest in that area?'

'Well, I suppose he was always rooting around second-hand bookshops when we went away somewhere. Or at least he was always wanting to. My mother discouraged him. She reckoned collecting books was a waste of time. And she didn't like dusty old books cluttering up the house.'

'But surely you saw the glass-fronted bookcase in the sitting room?'

'Oh yes. But I never really looked at what was in it.'

That seemed remarkably incurious to me. But all I said was, 'Maybe it was a hobby he concentrated on more after your mother died?'

'Maybe,' Roy said dubiously.

'Anyway, I've no experience in valuing that kind of stuff, so I thought I'd check with you.'

'Oh.' He sounded nonplussed. 'Maybe I'd better discuss it with Michelle.'

That didn't surprise me either. I'd already got the impression that Roy Waites was one of those men who rejoices in letting his wife run everything. Some feel threatened by female omnicompetence, some get a positive charge from it.

'Well, Roy, could you get back to me when you've talked to her?'

'Yes, of course. Or probably she'll call you. I've got quite a workload on at the moment.'

The last sentence didn't fool me. If he had no workload at all, it would still be Michelle who'd call me back. There was a decision involved.

'Incidentally,' I said, 'have you got a date for Cedric's funeral yet?'

I could have predicted the answer. 'Michelle's on the case,' Roy replied. 'Likely to be towards the end of next week.'

'Well, do let me know. I'd like to be there.'

'Why? You didn't know him that well, did you?'

'I'd like to be there,' I repeated firmly. 'I got very fond of your father during the last months of his life.'

'Very well,' said Roy, with the intonation of a shrug. 'We'll let you know when it is.'

'Thank you. And, with regard to the books, I thought what I'd do in the interim is to get back to the guy who sold them to Cedric – he seems to have used the same dealer most of the time – and ask for some sort of ballpark valuation figures from him.'

'I suppose you could.' He didn't sound too sure.

'It'd be a start.'

'Yes . . . I'll get Michelle to ring you.'

'Fine,' I said, with some level of resignation.

'Oh, incidentally,' said Roy, with a bit more animation, 'Michelle said you were lucky to have got the job.'

'I beg your pardon?'

'Clearing out Dad's things. Michelle had a call from another company, offering to take it on. And this other woman's rates were considerably less than yours.'

I felt pretty incensed. Although it wasn't my usual area of work, I had agreed to do the job because they'd asked me to. And I'd given them a discount on my usual charges. And now Michelle was whingeing about the agreement.

'What was the name of this other company?' I asked.

How did I know his answer was going to be 'BrightHome'? The apparition of Rosemary Findlay seemed to be stalking me.

'Well, enjoy your lecture,' I said drily. 'And I hope your students do too. I'll wait to hear from Michelle.'

I don't like men to be macho, but I do like them to have a vestige of a spine.

I had become intrigued by Cedric's book collection. The level of commitment in the way they were cared for – and indeed the amount of money he'd spent on them – made it even stranger that his son knew nothing about the obsession. I knew Cedric and Roy weren't close, but the situation still seemed curious.

I opened one of the books. *Stamboul Train* by Graham Greene. I took out the invoice. Bought after Flick's death. Cedric had paid quite a lot of money for it. To Augustus Mintzen.

Whose bookstore was in Petworth. And whose number was

on the invoice. I rang and fixed to see him the following day,
the Thursday.

I got my laptop from the Yeti and started listing the book titles.
Not the ones on the shelves. Only those Cedric had thought
worthy of the bookcase. The valuable ones.

While I was doing that, my mobile rang. It was Detective
Inspector Bayles. He wanted to come and talk to me about
Gervaise Palmier. My first reaction was that I didn't know anyone
of that name.

'Also known as Dodge.'

Yes, of course I knew he was really called Gervaise. I don't
think I'd ever known his surname.

'We haven't been able to contact him,' said the inspector, 'in
any of his usual haunts. And I wondered if you, Ellen, might be
able to help us locate him . . .?'

'I haven't seen him for a few days.'

'Ah. The thing is, he's someone we want to talk to as part of
our investigation into the death of Cedric Waites.'

NINE

Detective Inspector Bayles looked as avuncular as ever in my sitting room the next morning. But, having seen it before, I could now recognize the steeliness of purpose in his eyes.

'And, Ellen, Gervaise Palmier is vegetarian – is that correct?'

'Yes. Yes, he is.'

'I can't help noticing that you have a slight reaction each time I say "Gervaise Palmier". Am I to understand that you are unfamiliar with that name?'

'It's not what I call him.'

'Which is . . .?'

'"Dodge". It's a nickname.'

'Yes, I assumed it was. Not many "Dodges" you hear round the font these days. And, might I be reading too much into it . . . but did he get that nickname because some of the things he does are a bit . . . "dodgy"?'

'No, certainly not. It's just that . . . Do you really want me to explain?'

'If you wouldn't mind,' said the inspector implacably.

So, I went into an explanation of 'Diogenes Syndrome', also known as 'senile squalor syndrome', a condition of extreme self-neglect – and frequently hoarding – in the elderly. I explained it was named after the ancient Greek philosopher, Diogenes of Sinope, and it was in fact very unfair to him. He apparently lived in a large jar in Athens and was certainly not a hoarder. In fact, he was an extreme minimalist, and it was for that reason I had dubbed Gervaise with his name, later shortened to 'Dodge'.

The further I got into this narrative, the more ridiculous it sounded. And the inspector's expression showed that he shared that opinion.

'So, Gervaise is a minimalist?' he asked.

'Yes. Very keen on recycling. Won't let anything go to waste.'

'Admirable,' said Bayles drily. 'And do his green principles extend to vegetarianism as well?'

'Yes.' Then I couldn't stop myself from saying, 'But you really don't need to talk to Dodge. I know he was probably the last person to see Cedric Waites alive, but he can't have had anything to do with his death.'

'Possibly not, Ellen. But, as I told you when we last met, as a policeman, I start from very minimal knowledge. I have to work from the evidence I have. There's no sign of Gervaise Palmier – or Dodge, if you prefer – at his home, and no one seems to know where he's gone. But he knew that I wanted to talk to him. I left a message on his phone. In my experience, people who don't want to answer straightforward enquiries from the police usually have something to hide.'

'I don't think Dodge has anything to hide. He just has complex mental health issues.'

'"Complex mental health issues"?' the inspector echoed. 'Yes, we hear that quite often these days. But, in this case, the person in question also has a criminal record.'

Ah. Finally, I had confirmation of what I'd suspected for a long time. The breakdown Dodge had suffered in his late twenties had involved getting on the wrong side of the police. I thought the issue had probably been something to do with drugs. 'Can I ask what he has a criminal record for?'

'You can ask, but it's up to me whether or not I give you an answer. And, in this instance, I prefer not to. But when we add to the fact that someone doesn't want to talk to the police the additional fact that he has a criminal record . . . well, what started out as a minor suspicion becomes rather more substantial. Wouldn't you agree?'

'I can see how it could look like that,' I conceded. 'But, from what I know of Dodge, he's just very paranoid about any dealings with the police.'

'So are most criminals,' the inspector observed tartly. He smoothed his hands over his large belly. 'So, you have no idea where . . . Dodge . . . is?'

'No.'

'Apparently, he drives a rather distinctive vehicle?'

'Yes.'

'Could you tell me what that is?'

I felt like a captured agent shopping a complete spy network, but I couldn't pretend I didn't know. 'It's a 1951 Morris Commercial CV9/40 Tipper van. Painted blue.'

'You wouldn't know the registration?'

'I'm afraid I've never noticed.'

'No worries. We'll be able to track that down.'

And also, no doubt, be able to track Dodge down. I felt even worse, imagining his potential reaction to being cornered by the police. He was capable of getting himself into a whole lot more trouble.

'I believe your son works with him?' the inspector went on.

'Yes. Ben, he's called.'

'Right. And I dare say, as his mother, you'd have a contact for him?'

I supplied Ben's mobile number. Bayles thanked me and levered his large bulk out of the armchair.

'Inspector . . .?'

'Yes?'

'When you asked whether Dodge was vegetarian . . .'

'Mm?'

'. . . was it because the poison that killed Cedric was something plant-based?'

He looked at me ironically before saying, 'Ellen, contrary to the practice much featured in crime fiction of the more traditional type, we in the real police force tend not to share details of ongoing investigations with anyone who asks for them.'

I felt duly put in my place.

Petworth's a pretty little Sussex town, with more than its fair share of antique stores, non-chain coffee places, Range Rover Discoveries and Hermès scarves. Sort of place it'd be no surprise to find an antiquarian bookshop.

Augustus Mintzen's was in an old building just off the square. A low doorway, small shopfront with grey-painted wooden window frames, bulging slightly and asymmetric. Over the years I felt sure the shop had sold many things other than books.

I pushed the door open, activating an old-fashioned bell on a spring. That seemed almost too self-conscious a period detail, and it was of a piece with the shop interior. Books had been scattered with that artlessness which takes a lot of art to achieve. As a connoisseur of untidiness, I recognize calculated untidiness when I see it. There was something about the place that felt like a film set. This, it seemed to say, is what an antiquarian bookshop should look like.

The owner, when he appeared, maintained the theme. He looked like the sort of actor who would play an antiquarian bookseller in a movie.

But before he emerged, a woman hurried out from the stockroom or whatever lay at the back of the store. She was indeed wearing, tied over her hair, a Hermès scarf with a design of horse brasses. 'He'll be through in a minute,' she said as she brushed past on her way out to the street.

I had a fleeting sensation that she looked familiar, but my attention was quickly monopolized by the appearance of Augustus Mintzen himself. As I said, Central Casting could not have done better. He was probably only in his fifties but dressed to look older in a greenish tweed three-piece suit. He had a soft cream-coloured cotton shirt and a deliberately askew red tie. White hair curled around the fringes of a bald spot and continued into a fluffy beard. He wore a pair of tortoiseshell half-glasses, clearly used more as a theatrical prop than for seeing. Everything about him, to me, screamed phony.

And yet I know there are a lot of people who take comfort from fitting into the stereotypes of their profession. It's particularly noticeable in the medical world, where consultants take on the mannerisms of a previous generation, probably the generation who taught them. And patients respond to this illusion of the familiar. Everyone wants to be back in the world of Dr Finlay.

(It doesn't happen with declutterers. Ours is a relatively new form of employment, born out of the stresses of modern life. There is no previous generation for us to mimic.)

'Good morning. What can I do for you?' asked Augustus Mintzen. His voice, as I'd noticed on the phone the day before, was professorial, eccentric, slightly fuddled. Another part of the act.

'I'm Ellen Curtis.' For a moment, he looked at me blankly.

'We arranged for me to come to discuss Cedric Waites's book collection.'

'Ah yes. Yes, we did. Of course we did.' He looked around the shop. 'Did you bring the books with you?'

'No.'

'Oh? I thought you said you wanted me to give a valuation of them.'

'Yes, but since they were all bought through you, I thought you'd have a record of the transactions. I have a list, anyway.' I produced it from the back pocket of my jeans. 'And I've put down what Cedric paid for them.'

He looked at the sheet of paper dubiously. 'Of course, when valuing old books, their condition is often significant. A tear to a dust jacket can reduce the price by hundreds of pounds. So, without actually seeing the volumes in question . . .'

'All the ones listed here were sold to Cedric Waites within the last eight years. Their condition can't have deteriorated much in that time.'

'You'd be surprised . . . I'm sorry. I didn't take note of your name . . .?'

'Ellen Curtis. Call me Ellen.'

'Very well, Ellen. As I say, I'd have to see the books to give a realistic valuation. Things can deteriorate quite a lot in four years. And I gather that Cedric Waites lived in conditions of some squalor.'

I wondered idly how he knew that. 'Maybe, but he took punctilious care of his book collection. The ones on the list were kept in a special glass-fronted bookcase and dusted regularly.'

'Hm.'

'Did you ever meet, Cedric, Mr Mintzen?'

'No. He contacted me initially through my website and thereafter most of our correspondence was by email.'

Again, the implication that, at least at some point, the old man had had some kind of computer. I must try to root that out when I was next at 14 Seacrest Avenue.

'Did you ever speak to him on the phone?'

'A few times. Early on, I suggested delivering his books in person. He very much didn't want that to happen. Everything had to come through the post.'

That confirmed Cedric's status as a recluse.

'And, Mr Mintzen, do you know what prompted Mr Waites's interest in book collecting?'

'He told me it was something he'd wanted to do all his life but could never have afforded. His wife's death had given him the opportunity to follow his ambition.'

'Does that imply that he came into some money when his wife died?'

'I have no idea what it implies, Ellen. I was not cognizant of Mr Waites's financial circumstances.'

Again, Augustus Mintzen seemed to be playing the part of an eccentric bookseller. Does anyone in real life actually use the expression 'cognizant of'?

'I've done a rough tot-up of the figures here,' I volunteered, 'and I reckon we're talking thousands.'

Augustus Mintzen narrowed his lips in a sceptical intake of breath. 'Selling prices and repurchase prices can differ considerably, Ellen. The dealer obviously has to make some profit for the transaction to be worthwhile. And then there are other factors which can affect valuation considerably.'

'What "other factors"?'

'Where shall I start? Fashion is a big one. Author's reputations go up and down as fast as skirt lengths. Some minor writer languishes in post-mortem obscurity, then a feature film is made from one of his books and everyone in the world is suddenly desperate for a first edition.

'It works the other way too, of course. Authors drop out of fashion like stones. Particularly comparatively recent authors. For the sales of some, death is literally the kiss of death. Permanent fixtures in the bestseller lists . . . a few years after they kick the bucket, with no new title on the shelf, suddenly they feel very old-fashioned. Out of print in no time. Early twentieth-century fiction, the bottom's really fallen out of that market in the last few years.'

'Really?' This just sounded like salesman's talk to me. Surely it was no coincidence that my list of Cedric's books all fell into that category. He was softening me up for a very ungenerous valuation. And a hefty profit for himself.

I didn't feel any loyalty to Augustus Mintzen. I'd already

decided that, if I was charged with selling the books, I would do it through another dealer. So, I challenged him. 'You're just saying that, about early twentieth-century fiction.'

'What do you mean?'

'I don't believe that the value of Cedric Waites's collection has gone down noticeably in the last eight years.'

'Don't you?' He gave the full over-the-half-glasses stare. 'Then it's just as well that I'm the bookseller and you're not, isn't it? Because I actually keep an ear to the ground when it comes to the shifting popularity of deceased authors – and you clearly know nothing about it.'

I'd got as far as I was going to get with Augustus Mintzen. I picked up my list off his overcrowded desk and said, 'I must be on my way. Thank you very much for your help.' I hope he got the full impact of the ambiguity I put into the final word.

'My pleasure,' he said, apparently impervious to irony. Then, just before I reached the door, he stopped me. 'You're a declutterer by profession, is that right?'

'It is. Yes.'

'So, you must come across a lot of books when you're going through people's stuff?'

'I do.'

'Well, if you ever come across anything interesting that you're about to chuck out, give me a bell, eh?'

'How do you define "interesting", Mr Mintzen?'

'Unusual? Old? Possibly a first edition?'

'So, by "interesting", you mean "valuable"?'

'Yes, that's precisely what I mean,' he replied brazenly. 'Pity for stuff like that to end up at a car boot sale.' He seemed to read dissent in my expression. 'I'd give you a good price for them.'

Of course, that wasn't the reason for my potential argument. I was tempted to lash out with my response but curbed the instinct. I'd a feeling I might need to consult Augustus Mintzen again during my investigation. No point in parting on bad terms.

'Well, anyway,' he said, picking up a catalogue from the desk and handing it to me. 'Take this. You'll see my prices are very fair. Compare well with other dealers, both here and internationally.'

I took the catalogue, said a polite goodbye and left the shop.

And I wouldn't change my policy of giving excess books, which had to be got rid of, to Oxfam. If someone was going to make a profit from the rare valuable item, I'd rather it went to a good cause.

Certainly not to Augustus Mintzen. He hadn't taken long to join Michelle Waites on my list of people I wasn't prepared to think the best of.

When I got back to Chichester, I tried ringing Jools again. Still she didn't pick up. No surprise. She very often didn't pick up. And she was very dilatory in responding to voicemails. That's just how my daughter was. Mildly bolshie.

But Fleur's niggling had got me worried. I did something I rarely do and sent Jools a text.

I hadn't got any other appointments that day, so I did some work on my accounts. They tend to get done rather as and when. Maybe if I had a VAT number, I'd have to be more organized doing the quarterly returns, but I don't make enough money to be registered.

And yes, I do have an accountant, but I still have to get my invoices and expenses in order for her. Sometimes I think it'd be quicker and cheaper for me to do my actual accounts, but I'm not great at maths and would rather have the responsibility shared. SpaceWoman paperwork is the part of the job I don't enjoy, but I know it has to be done.

I was shuffling through, looking for an invoice that seemed to have disappeared, when my mobile rang. With excitement and a level of trepidation, I recognized the number as Tim Goodrich's.

He told me that he'd be getting the Deed of Probate for Cedric Waites's estate some time the following week. 'I've fixed an appointment with the solicitor for the Friday, tomorrow week. For me, Roy and Michelle.'

'The Reading of the Will?' I asked.

'I suppose that's what it will come to, yes.'

'Soon to be followed by the revelation of the document's contents to "other people"?'

He saw where I was going with this. '"Other people" being you again?'

'You read my mind, Mr Goodrich.'

'Hm.'

'Once the Deed of Probate is granted, the will becomes a public document. I could access it online.'

'True.'

'Though it would be simpler if the executor just told me the details.'

'Persistent, aren't you, Mrs Curtis?'

'Other authorities have observed that, yes, Mr Goodrich.'

'Very well,' he conceded with a cheerful sigh. 'As soon as I have the Grant of Probate, once I've told Roy and Michelle, you will be the next person to know.'

'Excellent.'

'Anyway, the point is that I'll be staying over in Chichester for the weekend. The funeral's going to be on the Monday after.'

'Ah. They said they'd let me know about that.'

'To be fair to them, I think they've only just got the date fixed. And there's still some question mark over it.'

'Why?'

'Maybe some problem about the police releasing the body . . .?'

'Ah.'

'Anyway, since I'm going to be in Chi . . .' He used the abbreviation like the local he once was '. . . I wondered whether you might be available for dinner . . . say, the Saturday . . .?'

I said I might.

I could no longer deny it. The prospect of seeing Tim Goodrich again was very attractive. He was very attractive. To me.

It was strange. Since Oliver's death . . . well, to be fair to the tact of my friends, since a couple of years after Oliver's death . . . I've had a lot of enquiries on the lines of 'Are you back in the dating game again?', 'Seeing anyone special?', 'I've found the perfect man for you – would you like me to set up a meeting?' And I've taken them at the level of banter. Yes, ho-ho, very funny, but in no way applicable to me.

I suppose I thought, sex, relationships . . . well, I've done all that. My involvement with Oliver was so all-encompassing that I had no expectations of another man in my life. Ever. And that was a future to which I was fully reconciled.

Sex was something I'd done in the past, like the netball I used to play at school. I'd enjoyed it at the time but never considered the possibility that it might be part of my life again. I certainly wasn't on the lookout for a local netball team to join. At my age? Though I was quite a useful Wing Attack in my day.

But Tim Goodrich . . . Yes, I fancied him. I was excited about the idea of having dinner with him the following Saturday.

It was a strange, unfamiliar feeling. But not an unpleasant one.

TEN

Another Sunday. Kenneth playing golf again. Fleur insisting on buying me lunch at Goodwood. Not ideal.

She'd ordered a bottle of Merlot before I arrived. That's kind of a concession to me, because she prefers to start lunch with white. But a whole bottle. She knows I'll only drink one glass. She'll finish the rest. No problem. And then drive the three or four miles back to Chichester. She won't get stopped by the police, of course. She never is.

Whereas I . . . I'm convinced if I were one milligram over the limit, the traffic cops would be magnetically drawn to the Yeti. I'd lose my licence. And, with it, SpaceWoman. There are not many things I'm paranoid about, but I'm afraid that's one.

I've seen my mother in many moods. She is an actress, after all. And I have to grant it to her, she can sparkle in company. When she's in animated, anecdote-telling mode, the years slip away and she naturally takes centre stage. I can recognize and remember the beautiful woman she once was.

When she's alone with the daughter she didn't much want in the first place, she makes no such effort. Her lips are permanently downturned in a rictus of martyrdom.

'Did you hear about Reggie Baldry?' she asked, after pouring my first (and last) and her second glass of Merlot.

'No.' I knew too well the reaction I'd get if I said, 'Who the hell's Reggie Baldry?'

'He died yesterday. At Denville Hall.' I knew that was a home for retired actors. 'We go back a long way. He was Florizel to my Perdita at Hornchurch. *Winter's Tale*, you know . . .'

I couldn't resist saying that I did actually know. Though I never made it to university, I am quite well read.

'Director, guy called Bill,' she went on, 'camp as a row of tents, he really fancied Reggie. And who wouldn't? Like a young Greek god he was then, Reggie. Bill couldn't keep his hands off

him. But I . . .' a sly smile '. . . got there first. He was very good
in bed, Reggie you know . . .'

Children are traditionally supposed to express revolted disbelief
at the idea of their parents having sex. To have one of them
boasting about her ancient conquests just adds another level of
embarrassment.

Fleur wound this up another notch by adding, 'Takes one to
know one.'

'So, Reggie's died,' I said. 'I'm sorry.'

'Oh, all the real actors are going now,' she moaned. 'The
generation who could bring whole theatres to life. The current
lot just don't have the scope; brought up mumbling their lines
for television cameras.'

Of course, I'd heard all this many times before. Was her view
in any way affected by the fact that, although she'd had her
successes on stage and in British films, Fleur had never really
conquered television? I was far too polite to ask.

'Not that anyone cares,' Fleur emoted on. 'One is just forgotten.
One's achievements are like so much dust under the wheels of
history.' I wondered from which of the plays she'd been in she'd
got that line.

'Age is cruel. One's sell-by date, like so much else, vanishes
into the past. No one really cares about the old. We're just the
flotsam and jetsam of a forgotten generation, washed up on
the shoreline of indifference.'

I wondered if that had come from the same play. But the signs
weren't good. Usually, Fleur resisted any suggestions that she
might be old. She'd spout that venerable line, 'You're only as old
as you feel', probably, after a snigger, adding. '. . . or as old as
the man you feel.' Or go into that 'age is just a number' routine.
But if she was actually talking about herself as being part of a
'forgotten generation' . . . it was going to be a long lunch.

'You just come to the point,' Fleur resumed, 'when you realize
that you're no use to anyone. Nobody rings you. You always
have to take the initiative if you ever want to see or talk to anyone
ever again. I mean, it's like with you, Ellen. Do you ever ring
me? No, I'm always the one who makes the call. Do you invite
me out for lunch? No, I'm the one who has to call you. It's
always been like that, hasn't it?'

This was so grotesquely unfair that I hadn't the energy to argue.

'And I thought,' Fleur continued, 'I had a close relationship with my granddaughter, but still no response when I contact her. Haven't you been in touch with her, Ellen?'

'No.'

'Well, aren't you worried about her?'

'Jools leads her own life. She'll be in touch when she wants to be in touch.'

'That may be true for you, Ellen, but I think the fact that she hasn't contacted me means there's something wrong. It's been over a fortnight since I've heard from her. I think you should go up to Herne Hill, Ellen, and find out what's going on.'

'I'm sure she's—'

'That's what anyone deserving of the name of a mother would do.'

That – from her? From Fleur Bonnier? Sometimes, when I think of Fleur Bonnier's behaviour towards me, matricide seems to be the only option.

I was still fuming when I got back home. And worried. Not worried about whether my booze-soaked mother had made it back safely to hers, but worried about Jools. Fleur's harping on about the subject had brought to the surface a number of long-buried anxieties about my daughter. The idea that I should go to Herne Hill to check Jools out, which before lunch had just been a passing fancy, now felt compelling.

And it stopped me from doing what another instinct prompted, namely to pour myself a second large glass of Merlot to obliterate memories of the lunch I had so recently endured.

My dithering was interrupted by the ringing of my SpaceWoman mobile. Detective Inspector Bayles. And in unnervingly jovial mood.

'Ah, Ellen. You remember our conversation agreeing that the police tend to be a little parsimonious with the amount of information about their investigations which they vouchsafe to the general public?'

'Yes,' I replied, wondering where this was going.

'Well, out of pure generosity of spirit and the goodness of my heart, I thought I'd vouchsafe you some.'

'Oh?'

'When we last spoke, you posited the idea that the poison which killed Cedric Waites might have been plant-based.'

'I remember, yes.'

'And I – perhaps churlishly, in retrospect – refused to confirm or deny your supposition.'

I didn't say anything. I was getting a bit tired of his elaborate storytelling routine.

Perhaps he was aware of my feelings, because he cut to the chase. 'The poison that killed Cedric Waites came from the oleander shrub.'

'I didn't know that was poisonous.'

'A lot of people don't, Ellen. But yes, the flowers or the leaves will do the business quite effectively. Used to be far more popular as a murder method than it is now. Victorians loved the stuff. Chemical poisons seem to have taken over these days. But, as I say, it works.'

'So?' I knew he had more to say.

'So . . .' He extended the monosyllable almost unbearably and then repeated it. 'So, when we inspected the home of your friend . . . Mr Dodge . . . we were interested to find some pots of oleanders.'

'He cultivates lots of flowers and herbs. Dodge uses them for his herbal potions.'

I shouldn't have added the second sentence. 'Yes, that's rather what we thought,' said the inspector. 'Which, taken in conjunction with his sudden disappearance – not to mention his criminal record – does . . . well, let's say it doesn't decrease our suspicions of Mr Dodge.'

'But, if growing oleanders makes someone a murder suspect, then you'd have to question half the gardeners in the country. Everyone has oleanders. There were some here when I bought the house. Winters here are too cold, so you have to bring the pots inside. But this time of year, mine are thriving outside.'

'Hm,' said the inspector wryly. 'So, you grow oleanders too, Ellen. That's very interesting.'

My anxiety about Jools was now getting out of control. It's that atavistic fear all mothers have when they think their child is in danger. It brought back the early panics when 'the baby isn't feeding properly', the terrified waits at St Richard's Hospital when 'we'd like to keep her in overnight for observation', the agony of tension which accompanied her first drive out on her own after passing her test. Nothing every other mother in the world hasn't experienced to a greater or lesser degree.

And certainly far more powerful and important than the idea that Detective Inspector Bayles might have me marked down as a murder suspect.

I rang Jools's mobile again. No reply, went to voicemail. I left a message which, while not I hope sounding totally manic, indicated that I would like her to call back as soon as possible. I backed that up with a text, and even sent a message to the email address I knew Jools hardly ever checked. (She had new, trendier communication platforms, ones I didn't know how to access.)

No argument now. I was going to drive to Herne Hill. I had a key to Jools's flat. I had to find out what had happened to her.

I wasn't driving at my best on that journey from Chichester up to London. Not going too fast, just my whole body was jumpy and twitchy. My hands trembled on the Yeti's steering wheel. Every gear change was a juddering risk. A lot of black looks were directed towards me by other road users in the end-of-weekend crawl back to the working week.

But I got to Herne Hill and parked outside Jools's building. I had been there a few times, but not as much as a mother in a more relaxed relationship with her daughter might have been. A lot when she first moved in, helping her get stuff together. Not many times since. On the last occasion, a window had opened briefly into her mind; that time she actually talked about Oliver and her reaction to her father's death. But the thaw had not been maintained. On the rare occasions when we did talk on the phone, her manner was as shallow and brittle as ever.

I didn't need Fleur's outrageous criticism to make me feel I hadn't done a great job as a mother.

I let myself in through the downstairs door into the tiny hallway. The place had been built as an Edwardian family house and turned into flats during one of London's (many) times of skyrocketing property prices.

There wasn't a lift. It would have taken too much valuable space from the flats the property developers wanted to sell at the highest price possible.

I tried to control my breathing and ease my tension as I climbed up the stairs. There was a bell-push by Jools's door. I pressed it, then pressed again. No reaction. I felt physically sick from the stress.

I opened the front door. Two steps took me to Jools's sitting room. I pushed that door open too.

The light was on. My daughter was lying on the sofa. She looked up in surprise at my entrance. She was as pale as the white wall behind her. She looked desperately frail and vulnerable.

Across her nose, strips of plaster held in place a gauze dressing, through which blood had seeped.

ELEVEN

I 've suggested that, after Oliver's death, conversation between me and my daughter didn't exactly flow. Well, in the Yeti back to Chichester that Sunday evening, she probably said as much to me as she had in all the intervening years added up.

And what she said made me realize how much the loss of her father had affected her. How much emotion she had been blocking out, how much had been building up inside. My preconception that I had a hypersensitive son and a daughter impervious to feeling was totally shattered.

Of course, it wasn't about Oliver that she talked, but everything she had done since his suicide, every decision she'd made seemed to have been motivated by the trauma of his death. As, in different ways, had been everything I'd done.

Jools had made no fuss when I proposed that I should take her back to Chichester. She was docile, almost in shock, seeming to welcome the fact that I had arrived on a rescue mission. Someone to take responsibility, to make decisions for her.

If I hadn't appeared, I don't know what she would have done. Her account was garbled, but I managed to piece together that she had been lying on the sofa for at least three days, eating nothing, just drinking tap water. She was in a kind of fugue state, having lost all energy and ambition.

She didn't argue as I changed the dressing on her nose. Under the bloodied gauze it was a horrible sight, a mass of cuts and bruises. I asked if she had hit the windscreen of a car, or if someone had beaten her up, but she wouldn't tell me what had caused the injuries. I let it rest. I didn't want to pressure her about anything.

It seemed, from what she said in the car, that her career in fashion was over. I blame myself a bit for having taken so little interest in what she actually did in that world. But she tended to flit off the subject when I asked about it. And I have to confess that the idea of instant fashion garments, destined for a couple of wearings on their way to landfill, went so much against my principles that I think Jools probably sensed my disapproval. At times I even wondered whether she had deliberately gone into that line of business to antagonize me.

But in the car it was all tearfully poured out to me, how my daughter's ambitions had been thwarted. For some of what she said, I almost needed an interpreter. There was a lot about social media and an online world of whose existence I was hardly aware.

'I was going to be an influencer,' Jools wailed. 'I was building up enough followers on Instagram – or I'm sure I would have done. And I was posting some really good videos on TikTok. And people were starting to take notice, I was getting lots of freebies from the fashion houses. It really was beginning to work.'

Pretending I understood more of this than I actually did, I asked what had gone wrong.

'People. Cruel people. Evil people.'

'What do you mean?'

'People started posting bad stuff about me.'

'On TikTok?' I asked hopefully.

'More on Twitter,' she replied.

'Ah.'

'Trolls,' said Jools. 'Threatening me, criticizing my appearance. Saying . . .' she sobbed '. . . that I was too ugly to be an influencer.'

'You shouldn't read stuff like that. Just ignore it.'

'I can't ignore it. Social media is what my work's about. I have to keep up to date.'

I said nothing. I couldn't argue with her conviction. And, knowing how much I had been hurt by the adverse Facebook review from Edyta Jankowski (whoever she might be), I hated to think what kind of online abuse Jools had suffered. My maternal protective instinct kicked in. How dare anyone criticize my daughter? I felt as riled and defensive as I had when some kid picked on her in the primary school playground.

'But now,' she confessed, 'I feel terrified what I'll find every time I go online.'

I somehow curbed my knee-jerk reaction: Well, don't bloody go online! It was time I found out what had happened to her face.

'But has it just been online, the violence? Or has someone attacked you physically?'

'What do you mean?'

'Your nose, Jools. What on earth happened to your nose?'

This prompted a new flood of weeping. When, eventually, I could work out what she was saying, it was apparently her nose which had attracted most vituperation from the online trolls. What they had said basically was that her nose was ugly. And no one with a nose like that had any chance of a career as an influencer.

Having got that out, Jools was assailed by a new bout of tears, through which the only word I could distinguish was 'Budapest'. This seemed so unlikely that I thought I must have misheard.

But no, when coherence returned, my daughter told me that she had just returned from a week in Budapest, where she had undergone plastic surgery. A nose job. In the hope that her looks would be sufficiently improved for her to have a future as an influencer.

This revelation prompted a range of emotions in me. Among them, a feeling of having been insulted. People always said Jools had got my nose.

By the time I delivered her to the house in Chichester, it was clear that a lot more was wrong with my daughter than a botched nose job. She was still as biddable as a docile child, incapable of making any decision.

Like a good mum, I sorted out food first. Nursery food. What she had liked to eat when she came home ravenous from school. Cheese on toast, with a layer of tomato ketchup between the bread and the cheese. I'd never liked it much myself, but that's what the ten-year-old Juliet had always wanted. The twenty-five-year-old Jools was equally appreciative.

She no longer wanted the after-school accompaniment of hot chocolate but was very happy with Merlot. While she ate and drank, I went upstairs to make up the bed in what I still thought of as 'her' room.

Then I ran a bath for her. The pre-teen Juliet had always liked

her bath before bed and still liked me to 'baby-dry' her up to
the age of eleven. Back then the bath would have been at about
six in the evening. This time, after the round trip to Herne Hill
and back, it was one in the morning.

And this time I did grant her the privacy of the bathroom to
herself, though in her dumbed-down state I doubt if she would
have objected to my presence.

I saw her safely into bed and I made her take a Zopiclone to
knock her out. I had some prescribed during those dreadful early
months after Oliver's death. They were well past their expiry
date, but I had taken one within the last year and it had worked.

Jools dropped off to sleep quite quickly, leaving her mother
to worry about the extent of her problems. I had a feeling there
was a lot more to come out.

I was right. The details emerged gradually over the next week,
as it became clear that my daughter was in the middle of a major
breakdown.

The first thing I did was to sort out her medical condition.
Face-to-face appointments at our local GPs' surgery are as rare
as hen's teeth these days, but I recaptured some of the fighting
spirit I'd had when the kids were small. My refusal to take no
for an answer resulted in my getting an emergency appointment
for that Monday morning.

Again, as if she was still a schoolgirl, I went in to see the
doctor with her. Jools made no objection to this. Once more, I
was struck by her passivity. It was such a change after the
combative way she had dealt with me ever since Oliver's death.

The doctor removed my improvised dressing from the injured
nose and was not amused by what she found there. She couldn't
be sure until the swelling went down, but she suspected that the
Hungarian surgeon had botched the job. When she asked how
much Jools had been charged for the work, the cheapness
prompted a sharp intake of breath and disapproving use of the
word 'unregulated'. She prescribed antibiotics to counter the risk
of infection and said she'd write a referral letter to a consultant
surgeon at St Richard's. But an appointment there would have
to wait until the swelling subsided.

A temporary dressing was put on Jools's face and I was told to go to the pharmacy to buy more of the dressings and change them on a daily basis. Somehow, instinctively, the doctor gave these instructions to me, acknowledging that, though my daughter was a grown woman, for the time being I was the one in charge.

I had cancelled all my Monday SpaceWoman appointments. There was nothing that couldn't be postponed. And I spent the day with my daughter. And found out, bit by bit, details of the fantasy world in which she had been living.

And how much it had all cost. And how many credit cards Jools had maxed out.

Increasingly, my main priority became keeping the news of her granddaughter's collapse from Fleur Bonnier.

Jools wasn't ill. Not in the physical sense, anyway. All right, she hadn't eaten any solid food for three days, but home cooking quickly restored her energy. She'd also slept a lot, day and night that Monday, cocooning herself in her duvet like she had when she was a little girl. In many ways she had reverted to childhood.

By the Tuesday morning, she was fit to face the world. Though what world she expected to face I had no idea. According to Jools, any career she might have had in the world of instant fashion was over for good. Whether she could keep on the Herne Hill flat, or whether her debts would mean she'd have to sell up, were questions which we hadn't embarked on yet.

But though my daughter's life seemed to be becalmed in a kind of docile torpor, mine had to continue. Postponing SpaceWoman commitments for one day was fine. Any longer and I'd have problems dealing with the backlog.

But I didn't want to leave Jools alone. This was a new experience for me. I was used to worrying about what my son was up to every minute of the day. With my daughter, I just assumed she was OK. Since Oliver's death, Jools had volunteered virtually nothing about her life and made me feel like a nag if I asked too many questions. If I asked any questions, actually. So, this was a complete reversal.

I didn't raise the subject until she emerged from her bedroom about nine on the Tuesday morning. I told her that I had an eleven o'clock appointment at Mim Galbraith's.

'And what are you doing there?'

'Tidying up some books for her.'

'Ah.'

'But the thing is, Jools . . .' I had a strong feeling that I should be calling my newly infantilized daughter 'Juliet', '. . . I don't really think I should be leaving you on your own.'

'I know what you mean,' she said. 'I'm not sure I want to be on my own.'

'No, but . . .' I hadn't expected to be faced with the problem of finding a babysitter in my fifties. 'I suppose I could—'

'Don't suggest I go to Fleur's!'

I was glad she felt the same way about that possibility as I did. 'I wasn't about to. But I could ring Ben and ask him if he's free to come over.'

'Does Ben even know I'm here?'

'I haven't told him.'

'Well, please don't. Not yet. I want to get my head together for a bit, then I'll talk to him.'

'OK. If that's what you want to do, fine.'

There was a silence. I really didn't want to have to ring Mim and postpone. In spite of her adventurous youth, she was now set in her ways. Change upset her. But, if that was what I had to do . . .

'Tidying up books,' said Jools suddenly. 'Doesn't sound too difficult.'

'No, it's not difficult, it's just part of what my job involves. Something that has to be done.' I spoke defensively. Previously, when discussions of SpaceWoman's usefulness had arisen, Jools had been firmly in Fleur Bonnier's camp.

'I can tidy up books,' said Jools. 'Can I come with you?'

I need not have worried about Mim Galbraith's reaction to my bringing 'staff' with me. She seemed to take an immediate shine to Jools. Maybe my daughter's comparative youth reminded the old schoolteacher of her former pupils. And her memory of their sensitivity about their appearance prevented her from commenting on the bandaged nose.

She offered us both coffee and, when Jools suggested she should go to the kitchen and make it, to my surprise, Mim agreed.

I hadn't said definitely that Dodge would be coming with me on this visit, but had prepared credible answers should the subject of his whereabouts arise. It didn't. Mim didn't mention him. Maybe she'd forgotten he'd been with me for my last visit.

It was strange having a helper at work. Since I started SpaceWoman, it had been very much a one-woman band. Oh, sure, I'd brought in Dodge from time to time when heavy lifting was required, and I'd been on the premises at the same time as my small army of heating engineers, electricians and so on (all of whose names began with 'D'), but I'd never had someone else working on the same job as I was.

I found it rather restful with Jools there. I even entertained the brief fantasy of our working together on a more permanent basis. I was increasingly having to say no to SpaceWoman enquiries because I was too busy. If I could spread the load between two of us . . .

I very quickly put a mental candlesnuffer on that idea. I had a feeling that Jools's current docility was a reaction to the trauma of her online sufferings. I couldn't see her staying that way. When the meek inherit the earth, my daughter won't get a share. Her innate bolshiness would reassert itself at some point.

But, for that brief time in Mim Galbraith's sitting room, we worked together harmoniously, dusting the books and separating them into piles according to their state of dilapidation.

And, while we worked, Mim kept up a more or less continuous monologue. I think, like a lot of the old, her basic problem was loneliness. Maybe, if she hadn't lived on her own, the dementia would not have made such inroads into her memory. Maybe not. But she certainly relished having an audience.

She didn't need prompts to talk, but the mention of an author or poet from her book collection rarely failed to produce an anecdote. When I observed that her Penguin edition of *Lucky Jim* was falling apart, she said, 'Oh, I thought I'd got a hardback. I did see a bit of Kingsley Amis just before it was published. With his wife Hilary. Well, his wife was Hilary then. I think he always had a roving eye, though. And the drink . . . God, I'm not sure that I ever saw him sober.'

A comment from me about her almost-complete collection of 'Penguin Modern Poets' reminded her that George MacBeth and

Edward Lucie-Smith were published in the same volume. On some details her memory was razor sharp. 'I met George MacBeth back then. I was sleeping with a friend of his, a less talented poet with an idiosyncratic attitude to personal hygiene. Poets are unreliable as a breed, not good for women who are looking for long-term security. Which, fortunately, I never was. There was somebody who started a literary club but wouldn't let poets join because, he said, "they drank too much, didn't pay their bills and went off with other people's girlfriends." Now who was it who said that? I know the name. It was . . . Oh, damn it, it's gone.'

And, once again, Mim Galbraith looked very old.

My recent visit to Augustus Mintzen and his brazenly asking me whether I'd scout out valuable books for him made me enquire whether Mim had ever been approached about selling some of her collection.

'No. Nobody knows I've got a collection. Anyway, I don't care about the value of my books. I don't want to keep them like bloody ingots in a bank vault. I want to read them. I want them to bring back memories of the first time I read them. Books are the continuity of my life. I didn't have children. The right time and the right man never coincided. I live through my books.'

I found it rather sad to hear her repeat verbatim what she'd said on a previous meeting. 'I was just wondering,' I said, 'if you'd ever heard of a book dealer called Augustus Mintzen?'

'I've never heard the name,' said Mim, in a manner which closed the conversation.

On the way back in the Yeti, after a long silence, Jools said, 'It's quite interesting, isn't it?'

'What?'

'Seeing real people.'

That prompted an even bigger 'What?' from me.

'Not just online,' said Jools.

I could see from her face reflected in the mirror that this was not the moment to follow up on what she'd just said. It was an expression I recognized from way back, when she was a toddler. Challenging and defiant. And I'd learnt early that far more effective than taking her on was waiting for the mood to change.

But what she'd said had raised disturbing images in my mind. Though she'd talked airily to Fleur about catwalk shows and collection launches, had Jools's entire career in the fashion industry been conducted online? Had my daughter, in a very different, contemporary way, been as much of a recluse as Cedric Waites?

That Tuesday evening, I had a call on the mobile. From Dodge.

'Where are you?' I demanded.

He didn't even bother answering that. 'Listen, I've been thinking, Ellen,' he said. 'About Cedric Waites being poisoned.'

'Yes?'

'Do you know what the poison was?'

'Yes. Detective Inspector Bayles told me.'

'Bayles? Was he the one who wanted to contact me?'

'Yes, he was. And he told me Cedric died of oleander poisoning.'

'Ah. I've got some pots of oleander back at my place.'

'Yes. He found them.'

'God, no. He's been to my place?' Dodge sounded very distressed. 'That'll make him even more suspicious of me.'

'What's making him suspicious of you is the fact that you've gone into hiding. If you go and see him, you'll be able to explain everything.'

'You reckon?' His voice was heavy with scepticism. 'The only thing that'll get me off the hook is to find definitive proof that I didn't poison the old boy.'

'And how do we find that?'

'I was thinking . . . given Cedric's track record for untidiness, it's quite possible that he left the containers for the last meals he ate lying around the house. So long as one of them wasn't one of the containers I prepared for him . . .'

I had to tell him. The awful truth, that I had personally destroyed the evidence which might have proved his innocence.

Dodge rang off. And I was no nearer knowing where he'd been ringing from than I had been at the beginning of the call.

I didn't feel good.

TWELVE

The following morning, the Wednesday, Jools seemed to take for granted that she would accompany me on my SpaceWoman rounds. I'd planned to spend most of the day continuing the clearance of 14 Seacrest Avenue, a job where it certainly helped having two pairs of hands.

I continued tidying downstairs while Jools dealt with Cedric's bedroom. Presumably, it was the room he had shared with Flick though, interestingly, they'd had twin beds. Jools started sorting out the clothes that would have to be chucked from those that might make it to the charity shops. There were very few in the second category. Clothes did not feature much in the old man's online shopping. He clearly wore the same things till they fell apart.

And, at some stage, he had removed all of his late wife's clothes.

Jools worked hard and seemed to have an instinct for what needed doing most urgently. She asked me for very little guidance. Again, I suppressed the seductive vision of the two of us working together in SpaceWoman. There was still far too much baggage, too many things between us, things that needed explanation. If I ever did achieve full rapprochement with my daughter, I knew it would be at the end of a long, long process.

I had to persuade her to stop working for a coffee break. I always have the makings of hot drinks amongst my permanent kit in the Yeti. Some clients may offer you a tea or coffee, many don't. And working in an empty property, you have to be self-sufficient. I always have a tin of that Nescafé Azera which tastes more like real coffee than most of the instants. And in Seacrest Avenue I used Cedric's kettle. (I did wonder again why the police hadn't shut the house off as a crime scene, why there wasn't plastic tape everywhere, but then all I know about how they work is gleaned from the unreliable source of crime series on the telly.)

'Nice collection of books in the sitting room,' said Jools as we sat, quite companionably, in the kitchen.

'Yes. It seems they were mostly bought since Cedric's wife died. Apparently, she wasn't interested in books.'

'They're very well looked after.'

'Obsessively well looked after. That's quite common with hoarders. There's one area of their life that's kept punctiliously tidy . . . and they never notice the chaos everywhere else.'

'Not that Cedric's chaos was too bad.'

'No, Jools. I've certainly seen a lot worse.'

'Hm. Funny. I've never really thought much about what you do, Mum.'

'No.' Well, at least she was honest.

'Must be strange, going into people's houses, shuffling through their rubbish.'

'You get used to it.'

'Hm.'

I didn't pursue the subject. Quite a moment, though. The first time my daughter had shown any interest in what I did for a living.

'One thing I've noticed that's odd . . .'

'Hm?'

'. . . is that Cedric didn't seem to have a laptop.'

I suppose that would seem particularly odd to someone who, apparently, conducted her whole life online.

'Or did you take it?' she went on. 'Did the police, come to that?'

'I don't know about the police. I certainly haven't seen a laptop anywhere here.'

'But there's a broadband router upstairs, which seems to be in working order.'

'Yes. And now I come to think of it, Jools, Cedric was keen that the broadband should be reconnected when I started sorting things out after his first fall.'

'Oh well . . .' My daughter shrugged. 'I guess the police would take a laptop if they found one, if they want to find out about the old man's contacts, that kind of thing.'

'Yes, they probably would.' I didn't mention how much more interested they might be if they thought Cedric Waites had been murdered. Jools needn't know about that. Not for a while, anyway. There was plenty of other stuff for us to talk about. 'Talk through' might be a more accurate expression. I was still reeling from the new information about my daughter that I had garnered in the last few days.

'I'll keep my eyes peeled, anyway,' said Jools. 'See if I can find a laptop somewhere here.'

I told her that I had an appointment elsewhere that afternoon. Gerry Cullingford, setting up his surprise for his wife Lita. I wasn't sure what I thought about that. Something in the set-up didn't quite ring true but I couldn't think what.

Jools could have continued tidying up at 14 Seacrest Avenue, but I was still uncomfortable at the idea of leaving her on her own. Knowing that I had a daughter with mental health problems was a new concept for me, but the history of Oliver and Ben made me wary.

'Couldn't I come with you?' she suggested. 'As part of the SpaceWoman team?'

'One of my staff of thousands?'

'Something like that.'

I had a thought. 'Hey. I've got a spare SpaceWoman polo shirt in the Yeti. Do you fancy wearing the livery?'

'You bet!' She grinned, looking suddenly as she had when she was five years old.

She put the shirt on gleefully. No freebie she'd got from a fast-fashion designer, I felt sure, could have put an equivalent beam on to her face (definitely visible behind its surgical dressing).

We went to a café I'd noticed round the corner from Seacrest Avenue and had bacon sandwiches for lunch, sitting side by side in our matching polos. I was just wiping a paper towel round my greasy lips when the mobile rang.

'Hello. SpaceWoman.'

'Ellen, it's Gerry Cullingford.'

'Oh, hi. I hope you're expecting us.' Funny, how easily I said 'us' rather than 'me'.

'Well, that's the thing,' he said. 'I was here, ready to greet you, and Lita walked in. Completely unexpectedly. And, as I said, what I'm doing is a secret. She's just out of the room for a moment. So, look, can we reschedule? Oh, hi, darling.' This greeting was not for me. And then, just before he switched off the phone, I heard Gerry Cullingford say the lie beloved of adulterous husbands everywhere, 'Wrong number.'

The call did not reduce the uneasiness I felt about the Cullingfords. I explained to Jools that the appointment was off.

'Pity. I feel like striding in somewhere in my SpaceWoman kit.'

'Well, we can stride back to Seacrest Avenue, I suppose. Get on with the clearance job.'

'Yes. I'm still convinced I'm going to find a laptop there.'

'Wish you luck.'

'It's just a matter of thinking myself into the mind of a recluse, in his late seventies,' said Jools. 'Think like him and then I'll find his laptop.'

I liked her approach to a problem. It mirrored my own. First understand the person, then you begin to understand the behaviour.

But our return to 14 Seacrest Avenue was delayed – as it turned out, prevented – by another call on my mobile. Gerry Cullingford again.

'Listen,' he said. 'Lita's gone out now. So, if we could still keep the appointment we arranged . . .?'

'All right,' I said, grinning across at Jools, 'I'll be bringing my assistant with me.'

The garage had changed considerably since I last saw it. One thing there was no sign of was an electric car.

I mentioned this to Gerry Cullingford, a bluff, hearty man who wore the kind of leisurewear that looked as if it was for going sailing, but which nobody who'd ever been in a boat would wear.

'Oh, I'm afraid that's Lita all over,' he said. 'Keeps changing her mind.' He raised his eyes to the heavens. 'Women, eh?'

Possibly not the most appropriate thing to say to the combined staff of SpaceWoman. I looked around the garage space. It was a lot tidier than when I last saw it. There were two tables and a couple of chairs. On one of the tables stood an expensive-looking sewing machine. There were bolts of cloth and other needlework impedimenta on a row of shelves.

'Lita wants all this moved out,' said Gerry.

'Really? Why?'

'Another of her fads,' he said. 'They never last long. She got all this lot set up, was determined to make a business of designing clothes. Couple of days behind the sewing machine and she'd had enough. Her next idea is she's going to learn the clarinet.'

'So, if I do clear this lot out, what do you want me to do with it?'

'Lita said my stuff you gave to charity.'

'Some of it.'

'Hope my golf clubs went to a good home.'

'They did, actually. A very good home. They'll be helping some deprived kid get an interest in life.'

'Well, that's good. That's what I like to hear.' He gestured round the garage. 'So, can you do the same for this lot?'

'Give it all to charity?'

'That's right. That's what Lita would want to happen to it.' The grin with which he said this was almost conspiratorial.

It made me feel uncomfortable. There was something very odd going on in the Cullingford household. I didn't know what it was, but I knew I didn't want to be part of it.

I said I didn't really do that kind of disposal of goods. I was a declutterer and the contents of the garage were far too well organized to qualify as clutter.

Gerry was disappointed but soon realized I wasn't going to change my mind. As he saw us off the premises, he said, 'Send us an invoice.'

I said I would and I meant it. Charge my top rates, too. Nothing annoys me more than having my time wasted.

'What on earth was all that about?' asked Jools, once we were back in the Yeti.

'I've no idea. I think it might be some elaborate game he and his wife are playing. Not a game I want to be involved in, anyway. I'm afraid you encounter a lot of time-wasters in this business.'

As you'll find out if you join me in it. I'd been within an ace of saying the words out loud. Thank God I stopped myself. But there was something about sitting there with my daughter, in our matching polo shirts, which was powerfully attractive.

Fortunately perhaps, I was moved off that train of thought by the arrival of a text.

'Ma,' it read, immediately identifying the sender, 'Pippa's away for a few days. OK if I stay at your place? Hope so because

I'm actually here. A few thoughts on where Dodge might be. Love, Ben.'

No problem, of course, about him staying. But I still felt I should go back home rather than to Cedric's. I still needed to cover any unexpected move from Ben.

Wow, my daughter and my son together in the same house. When had that last happened?

'Sister mine!' Ben shrilled fulsomely, as he embraced her in a bear-hug. Then he drew back and took in her polo shirt. 'Ah. I see that you have been subsumed into the SpaceWoman cult. Beware, it is a sect from which there is no escape.'

Jools giggled. She has a very distinctive giggle. I couldn't remember when I'd last heard it.

'Can I get you both something to drink?' I asked. 'I'm going to have a coffee.'

'I've got rather hooked on Dodge's nettle tea,' said Ben wistfully. 'I don't suppose . . .?'

'You don't suppose correctly,' I said. 'Ordinary Builder's?'

'That'll have to do, Ma.'

'Jools?'

'Could I possibly have . . . hot chocolate?'

The regression to childhood was complete. Hot chocolate had been Juliet's go-to drink on every occasion – she even asked for it when we went on family outings to pubs – until . . . well, until Oliver's death, I suppose. When so much else in our lives changed.

I should have been relieved at hearing my son and daughter chattering away in the sitting room while I was in the kitchen making their drinks, but my dominant feeling was anxiety. I had seen Ben – as I had seen his father – in this brittle, jokey mood before. It never boded well. The fragile high was almost always followed by a desperate low.

I wondered what his words about Pippa 'being away for a few days' meant. Maybe no more than that. But my instinctive maternal fear was going into overdrive. Had my perfect son's unsuitable girlfriend had the nerve to dump him?

I took the drinks in and sat with them while we drank. The full family of three. Feeling quite cosy.

But, before settling into the cosiness, I needed information from Ben. 'You said you had some ideas about where Dodge might be . . .?'

'Yes. There are a couple of people, friends of his, who I've met when they came to the workshop. Might be worth asking them.'

'But you haven't asked them yet?'

'I will, Ma, I will.'

His tone made me sound as if I'd been nagging him. Which was not my intention. I was just desperate to get Dodge back to his relatively ordered life of recycling and renovation.

'I've got numbers for them,' Ben went on, 'though whether they still work I don't know. They're not the most reliable sort of people.'

That didn't sound good. Dodge did voluntary work at a drug rehabilitation centre. If he'd been looking to some of his clients there to shelter him . . . I always worry about people who've had drug problems getting too deeply involved with other users. Dodge in his normal routine wouldn't be at risk, but a Dodge fearful of being hounded by the police . . . who could say what extremes he might resort to? The thought of him starting to use again . . .

'I'll talk to them soon,' said Ben. Adding, 'Promise, Ma.' Which again made me sound like a bit of a nag.

It struck me that Ben had shown no surprise at his sister's arrival at the house with me, although he could have had no inkling that she was in Chichester. Nor did he make any comment or ask any questions about the injury to her face.

I wondered, almost with a feeling of paranoia, whether they knew all about each other's lives. Both of them spent a lot of time on their computers. Making contact with people, presumably? Would it be so strange if they were actually making contact with each other as well?

Communication between a sister and brother could easily bypass their mother. In fact, that would probably be the more common scenario than all three sharing everything. And what could be better served by social media than exchanges between two siblings about the inadequacies of their mother?

I was determined not to take up the Fleur Bonnier default position and feel martyred. My daughter and my son seemed to be getting on well together. That was all that mattered.

Ben turned to Jools. 'So, sister mine, how have you been these long years? Living up the life of the London fashionista.'

'Of course,' she replied. 'Can't you tell from the polo shirt?'

They both chuckled at this, which didn't reduce my unease.

'And you, brother mine,' asked Jools. 'Being an innovative animator or making furniture – which one's the day job and which one's the hobby?'

'Furniture's the day job. Animation is definitely just a hobby.'

'Oh, you say that,' I intervened, 'but in fact your *Riq and Raq* film is up for an award this very weekend and—'

'Will you not bloody mention it!' Ben shouted at me. It felt like a physical slap. He had never shouted at me before. 'That's what bloody Pippa kept doing! She wouldn't leave it alone, kept on about it. That's why we . . .' He corrected himself before he said it. 'Why she's gone away for a few days,' he concluded limply.

As he turned back to Jools, the anger in his voice was replaced instantly by boyish charm. 'So, tell me, sister mine, what salacious stories can you tell me of your adventures in the dating game?'

I had often wanted to ask the same question – though I might not have put it in those words – and I awaited her response with interest.

But both mother and brother were doomed to disappointment. 'Quite honestly, Ben darling, being a fashionista makes me such a busy bunny that I don't have time for dates.'

The evasiveness – and the fact that she'd dropped back into the bantering manner she always used when she was with Fleur – made me think that my two children might have a more revealing talk without a mother's presence on the scene.

I said I had some shopping to do and left them to it. They hardly seemed to notice my departure.

When I said I had some shopping to do, it was true.

Strange how you don't notice change if it happens gradually. It's like elderly couples not realizing that, to the outside world, they look old. To each other, the minor depredations of the years have happened so relatively slowly, they're almost imperceptible. Unfortunately, Oliver and I were never able to put that process to the full test.

Anyway, it was the same with the contents of my knickers drawer. Yes, knickers and bras got replaced when they split or got noticeably frayed. But otherwise, they went through the regular cycle of being worn, placed in the dirty clothes basket, going through the washing machine, going through the tumble dryer and being worn again. It was very rarely that I actually thought what they looked like. And the concept of wearing matching bras and knickers never went through my head.

But in the last week I had found myself actually seeing my underwear as someone else might see it.

Now, I hasten to add that this was just a random thought. Maybe my forthcoming dinner with Tim Goodrich had got me thinking how I might feel if the occasion was a date. But I knew full well that it wasn't a date.

Nonetheless, I did select my new bras and knickers with considerable care. Thinking about colours, I avoided those skin tones which always make me think of surgical appliances. And white somehow felt too bland and obvious. Other primaries felt risky and somehow not me. Red? No. Was that a reaction to everything I'd read about Scarlet Women? And the pastels looked a bit wishy-washy. I homed in on black.

Not skimpy. Just well cut, on classic lines. Comfortable.

I have to admit actually buying the stuff did feel mildly transgressive. Only mildly, though. We are talking M & S here, not Ann Summers.

As I walked back home, I was thinking about my changed circumstances. Having two children at home is what I mean. Calling them 'children' actually feels daft. But the English language, usually so deft and flexible, hasn't come up with a decent word for grown-up offspring. So 'children' will have to do.

And children, both of whom had problems. I was used to worrying about Ben. Worrying about Jools was a novelty. And the fact that it was a novelty made me feel guilty. I should have monitored my daughter's life more since she'd been in London. Shouldn't have been put off by the barricades she had built up around herself. Shouldn't have assumed that no news was good news.

With that anxiety came a new one. Fleur Bonnier. I hadn't heard from my mother since I last saw her on the Sunday, but the weekend was once again looming and it was only a matter of time before she called me. Kenneth would once again, inevitably, be playing golf on Sunday, which would guarantee a request for me to join Fleur for lunch at Goodwood or an ill-disguised plea for me to invite her to my place for lunch. Which would inevitably involve either her seeing her granddaughter or, at the very least, being given some information about recent events in her granddaughter's life.

I would have to talk to Jools. As I thought of her I wondered, no doubt unrealistically, about the chances of her ever reverting to calling herself 'Juliet'.

I was so deep in thought that the ringing of my mobile was almost a shock.

'Hello? SpaceWoman,' I said. Daytime calls on that number were usually work.

'Ellen, hello.' I was amazed how instantly I recognized Tim Goodrich's voice.

'Oh, hi. Good to hear you.' Sudden anxiety. 'Are we still OK for the weekend?'

'Yes. Absolutely fine. At least I am.' Then perhaps he had a matching moment of anxiety. 'I hope you're not going to tell me you can't make it.'

'No. I'm fine too.'

'Glad to hear that. I'm really looking forward to it.'

'Me too.' Damn. Shouldn't have said that. Just slipped out. Dangerous to sound too keen. I'm sure that was one of the rules back in the days when I used to go out with boys. Frankly, that time seemed so long ago, I couldn't remember the moves of the dating square dance.

'I was actually ringing to firm up the details,' said Tim. 'I've booked us a table for eight o'clock Saturday evening at the Chichester Harbour Hotel. I'm staying there again,' he added.

'Fine,' I said, wondering whether there was a subtext there. And not too worried if there was.

'It'll be nice to see more of you,' he said. Another remark which could have contained a subtext. Which again I didn't resent. I was, after all, walking home carrying an M & S carrier full of new underwear.

'Incidentally,' Tim went on, 'we've got the Order of Probate on Cedric's will.'

'Oh yes. You hoped you would have by now.'

'Which means that the will is now a public document and I can talk about its contents.'

'Oh?' I said, sounding casual but hoping desperately that he would continue the conversation in the direction I wanted.

He did. 'Makes quite interesting reading.'

Another apparently non-committal 'Oh?' from me.

'Cedric's entire estate is divided between two people.'

He was playing now, deliberately building up the tension, so I didn't give him another prompt.

'And those two people,' he went on, 'are, interestingly enough, not Roy and Michelle.'

'Really?'

'They get absolutely nothing.'

'Wow. I can't see Michelle taking kindly to that.' My instant thought was what would happen to the two thousand pounds she'd taken from her father-in-law's bedroom.

'No, nor can I. And Roy, of course, will feel whatever she tells him to feel about it.'

'Yes. Do they know yet?'

'No. They're due in Chichester Friday. I thought I'd tell them face to face.'

'I don't envy you that encounter.'

'Really? I'm quite looking forward to it,' he said with some relish. 'Though not as much, of course, as I'm looking forward to seeing you on Saturday night.'

'You silver-tongued devil.'

'Yes, I am a bit of one, aren't I?'

'So, come on, tell me.'

'Tell you what?' he asked in mock innocence.

I spelled it out. 'Who are the two beneficiaries of Cedric Waites's will?'

'Oh,' said Tim, playing out his denouement. 'Vi Spelling . . . and me.'

THIRTEEN

As I've probably made over-clear by now, it was a very long time since I had thought of a man in a sexual way. But there was absolutely no doubt that was how I was thinking about Tim Goodrich. And I didn't think I was flattering myself to believe he shared my feelings. 'You'll know when it happens,' my girlfriends would tell me at the end of drunken evenings when I had resolutely insisted on my lack of interest in any such entanglements.

And now I think it had happened and I did know. My buying the new underwear – even if it was only M & S – was an indicator from me. And Tim's deliberately booking dinner at the hotel he was staying in was an indicator from him.

It all felt pretty simple. And I didn't feel any guilt. There was none: What would Oliver have thought? I was a grown-up woman, possibly opening up a new chapter in my life.

Two worries did remain, however. One was the state of my body, which I had hardly given a thought for the last few years. I suppose Oliver was the last man to see me naked and, in the time since then, I had knocked off a quick – and, mercifully, not too disruptive – menopause. That was another thought, actually. I would no longer have to worry about having an inconvenient period – or indeed getting pregnant. All that seemed a long, long time ago.

But, although I hadn't spent time chronicling and bemoaning every new line and wrinkle on my body, I knew there must be some. Hmm . . .

I'd steel myself to looking in a mirror when I tried on the new underwear.

The other worry made me feel rather stupid. At almost any other time since Oliver's death, I could have returned in the small hours or spent the whole night away from home without anyone either knowing or caring. This Saturday, both my children would be in the house.

It was all the wrong way round. Parents worrying about what sexual shenanigans their children are getting up to is a common enough experience. Parents hiding their amorous activities from their children is a whole different ball game. And a rather embarrassing one at that.

Seaside towns have an inherent tackiness. Attempts at gentrification in them never seem to be completed. With some, this contributes to their charm. There's an appealing loucheness about Brighton or Hastings or Littlehampton. The ones that have declined from fashionable grandeur, like Bognor Regis or Folkestone, are just sad. But the most depressing areas are to be found in seaside towns with a naval history. Like Portsmouth.

Which is where I was on the Saturday morning with Ben. After some sustained good weather, it was raining heavily, which only made the drab streets more dispiriting.

But the mission we were on should have been cheering. Ben had managed to make contact with one of Dodge's 'friends' and the fact the man had agreed to meet us raised the possibility that we would soon find the fugitive. Then, hopefully, convince him that he had nothing to fear from the police. Though I couldn't announce that they'd found out who poisoned Cedric Waites, I still had confidence in my powers of persuasion if I saw Dodge face to face.

I had been in two minds about leaving Jools on her own. But, though she currently had serious mental health issues, I didn't have the same worries with her as I had with Ben. She was certainly in a strange state but not suicidal. Now she had got over the days of weeping that had started the week, she appeared very rational, even serene. I hadn't dared ask for details about the extent of her debts and the collapse of her career. Indeed, I found myself doubting how much that career had ever existed. Had it all been some online fantasy? But explanations for all that could wait.

When Jools volunteered to continue the tidying-up job at 14 Seacrest Avenue, I thought that was a really good idea. She had caught on very quickly to what the task required. And though I tried not to work at weekends, if Jools wanted to, good for her.

That elusive fantasy of my collaborating with my daughter in SpaceWoman wouldn't quite go away.

Ben was still as tight as a coiled spring, but I think glad to be distracted by a visit to Portsmouth. I knew what was biting him but, remembering the outburst my enquiry had prompted the day before, was too canny to mention the TOCA Award. I also knew there was no chance of my son's mood settling until the result were made public that evening. He had let slip that would happen at around eight o'clock Italian time, an hour earlier here.

I understood how much this thing meant to him. Winning the award would offer a validation, a pointer to the future. It would place him in the ranks of professional animators and show the possibility of a career path opening up. Then, in time, one day Ben might be able to tell his sister that his day job was animation rather than furniture-making.

With those thoughts, though, came the fear of how he might react if he didn't win. His current feverish sparkiness was not a good omen. I had the seen the consequences of such moods too often with Oliver.

'Pat's a nice guy,' said Ben, referring to his Portsmouth contact. 'Really rates Dodge. You could tell. When he came over to the workshop, he said he owed Dodge a lot. Said he owed him his life perhaps.'

I can imagine that. Dodge would do anything for anybody else. It was only himself he despised and neglected.

'So Pat was someone Dodge had met through his drug rehabilitation work?'

'Must've been. Not that Dodge ever said anything about it. He never mentions that stuff.'

'No.' I wanted to ask Ben whether he'd been given any more information than I had about the circumstances of Dodge's breakdown, but I bit back the temptation. If Dodge had wanted me to know more detail he would have told me. If he confided more in my son, well, that was up to him.

As per instructions, I'd parked the Yeti at the end of a row of dilapidated lock-ups, brick arches that had once supported some defunct railway line. There was a lot of rubbish around, in the distance a blackened oil drum which probably, in colder

weather, hosted impromptu fires. I felt sure, when we got out
of the car, our feet'd be crunching on the detritus of syringes.

I looked at my watch. 'He did say half past ten, didn't he?'

'Yes, Ma.'

'It's quarter to eleven.'

'He'll come. As I think I said, his type are not the most
reliable.'

'No.'

'Ah. That's him, Ma.'

A dangerously thin young man had just ambled round the
corner towards us. He wore grubby jeans and a faded T-shirt
advertising a tour by some defunct rock band. Ben got out of
the Yeti and stood on the pavement to greet him.

'Hi, Pat.'

'Hi.'

I joined them. 'My mother, Ellen,' said Ben.

'Hi,' said Pat. 'Dodge talked a lot about you.'

'Really?' It was hard to imagine Dodge talking a lot about
anything.

'He trusts you. Otherwise, I wouldn't be doing this.'

'You know where he is?' I asked urgently.

Pat nodded. 'He made me swear not to tell a soul, but I'm
worried about him.'

'Is he ill?'

'Not in his body . . .'

I nodded. 'I know what you mean. Needs help?'

'I reckon, yes. He's in a bad way. Seems to be seeing things.
Having hal-hal- . . . what's the word?'

'Hallucinations?'

'That's it, yes.' Pat looked worried. 'Dodge is going to be well
angry that I've told you where he is. But, like you say, he needs
help.'

'You're doing the right thing, Pat. You know you are.'

'Yeah. Dodge's done so much for me, I feel I've got to help
him.'

'You have to, yes. Have you been taking food to him?'

'No, he says he's got stuff.'

I wouldn't have worried if it'd been anywhere else. Put Dodge

in the middle of the countryside and there's no one better at
foraging. But in the seedy back streets of Portsmouth . . .

'All right,' I said. 'Where is he?'

Pat jerked his head in the direction of the lock-ups. Ben and
I followed him in silence till he stopped outside one whose paint
had almost all been worn away. Rainwater pooled in front of it.
There was a narrow, uneven gap between the double doors. The
rusted accumulation of padlock hasps and staples on their sides
maybe bore witness to the number of times the place had been
broken into.

Pat had a key to the one functioning padlock.

'Is he actually locked in?' I asked.

'Yes, but he can reach this to let himself out. Don't think he's
done that much, though. Been lying low.'

Pat neatly undid the padlock and, before opening the sagging
doors, whispered to Ben, 'Be on your toes in case he tries to
make a dash for it.'

With that, he swung the doors outwards, to reveal the very
welcome sight of a familiar blue 1951 Morris Commer CV9/40
Tipper van.

Of Dodge, though, there was no trace.

Maybe he'd somehow got an inkling of our planned rescue
mission. Or maybe he was just reacting to his mounting
paranoia.

Either way, he had once again done a runner.

The atmosphere when we got home could have been more
relaxed. I knew why Ben was bouncing off the walls. I didn't
know how he would hear about the TOCA Award results. It was
far too low-key an occasion to be televised, but no doubt there
was some online service that would report the winners and losers.

He couldn't settle to anything. Hardly touched the late bacon-
and-egg lunch which I made when we got back from Portsmouth.
Kept disappearing upstairs, then coming down again, switching
the television on to watch random bits of sport (and Ben had
absolutely no interest in sport).

I knew and understood his tension. But I didn't say or ask
anything, for fear of getting my head bitten off again.

Anyway, it was all right for Ben. He had an acceptable reason for being twitchy. How could I explain my matching twitchiness without saying too much? Neither Ben nor Jools had shown much interest when I said I was 'going out for dinner with a friend'. But it was hard to hide my bubbling anxiety and excitement about the forthcoming encounter. And I still hadn't checked out my aging body in the mirror.

Fortunately, I was distracted mid-afternoon by a phone call.

'Hello. It's Vi Spelling.'

'Hi.'

'I hope you don't mind me ringing, but something rather odd has happened.'

'Oh?'

'I've been remembered in Cedric Waites's will.'

'Ah.' Better keep quiet about the fact that I already knew.

'And I was just wondering . . .'

'Yes?'

'Whether you had too.'

Vi definitely wanted to talk. She was coming into the centre of Chichester to do some Saturday afternoon shopping and readily accepted my invitation to drop in for a cup of tea. It would be a welcome distraction for me and, though my mind was full of Tim Goodrich, I did still want to solve the mystery of Cedric's death. If he was leaving Vi Spelling half of his estate, then maybe they'd had a closer relationship than she had implied.

She clearly found my house intriguing. Maybe she found all other people's houses intriguing. I got the impression Vi didn't have much of a social life. And remembered, of course, that she'd spent so much time looking after her reclusive brother, Clark.

She was excessively grateful for her tea and, when I produced biscuits, confessed to a sweet tooth. I laid off them myself, anticipating a good dinner at the Chichester Harbour Hotel. The thought of that made me suddenly and inexplicably worried that, come the evening, I might not be able to eat anything. Most peculiar, not like me at all.

'Anyway,' said Vi, comfortably settled into one of my armchairs, 'the reason I asked whether you got anything in Cedric's will was because it seemed so unlikely that he'd leave me anything. I didn't do much for him, you know, just cook the odd meal. You did more, what with all the tidying-up after he had his fall.'

'Not that much. Anyway, he didn't leave me a thing. And I certainly wasn't expecting anything.'

'So where does the rest of the estate go?'

Since Cedric's will was now a public document, I couldn't see any reason not to tell her that her co-inheritor was Tim Goodrich.

'The executor?'

'That's right.'

'So, Roy and that ghastly wife of his . . .?'

'Get nothing.'

'That's a bit of a slap in the face, isn't it?'

'Such a slap in the face that it must have been deliberate. Cedric was making a point.'

'Well . . .' The old woman rubbed her chin thoughtfully. 'I can see why. They never came to visit him. One measly phone call a month . . . I wouldn't call that caring for a parent. Would you?'

'No.'

'When I think how I looked after my mum and dad till they passed . . . And I'm not giving myself a pat on the back here, because I loved them to bits and I wouldn't have had it any other way. But, you know, it did take a lot of time, took a lot of my life. Most of it really,' she added wistfully, 'if you include what I done for Clark.'

There was a silence. Then, with a change of tone, Vi went on, 'I didn't know I was going to get this. This inheritance. I never knew about it till the executor . . . Tim Goodrich . . . rang yesterday.'

'No,' I said. 'No reason why you should have known.'

'It's just . . . if people talk . . .'

'What do you mean?'

'Well, there's talk going round that Cedric was poisoned.' Yes, of course, the rumour mills of Chichester must've been working overtime. 'And people know that I did food for him and they might think, if I knew I was going to inherit something, well . . . that I might have hurried him on his way.'

I was going to argue that nobody would think that, but I knew how, in a small city like Chichester, they probably would. So, I just said, 'You shouldn't worry about it.'

'Well, I . . .' She looked uncertain. 'I think Cedric was very disorganized with his food. Everything was shoved in the freezer, in any old order, and he just grabbed something when he felt hungry. I don't think he was particularly worried about "best before" dates.'

'No, I don't think he was.'

'So, he could easily have got poisoned by something that had just been left in there too long.'

'Yes, he could. On the other hand, he must have defrosted the freezer from time to time. Otherwise, it would have just seized up and stopped working.'

'Hm. Anyway, people are saying that it wasn't that. They're saying it wasn't accidental, that someone did deliberately poison him.'

'I've heard that rumour too.' I didn't want to worry Vi even more by bringing the police into the discussion.

'But I don't like it,' she persisted, 'the thought that someone wanted to kill Cedric.'

'It's not a nice thought, I agree. But, honestly, Vi, you don't have to worry. Nobody would ever imagine that you had anything to do with it.'

'No.' She sounded partially, but not wholly, reassured.

'And there's nothing else you saw . . . you know, as a neighbour?'

'How do you mean?'

'Anyone unexpected going to Cedric's house?'

'Well, he wouldn't let anyone in, would he?'

'No, but I was wondering whether you'd seen anyone trying to make contact, knocking on his door or . . .'

'Oh, I see what you mean.' She thought for a moment. 'No, can't remember anyone.'

'If you do think of anything – or anyone – do let me know.'

'Of course.' There was a silence. 'I don't know what I'll do with it.'

'With what?'

'The money. My inheritance. I've no use for it now. My pension covers everything I need. Mind you, if I'd got the money forty years ago, I don't know what I couldn't have done with it.'

Her eyes glazed over as she looked forward to the future. Not a very long future, after a lifetime of unrealized ambitions.

Round half past six I got dressed for the evening. I'd decided earlier in the week what to wear and I didn't allow myself to be sidetracked by other possibilities. I put on the new underwear automatically and then the trousers and top. It was only when I was doing my make-up that I realized I hadn't done my promised look at my body in the mirror. Probably just as well. No need to frighten the horses.

It was just before seven when I finished. It'd only take me ten minutes to walk to the Chichester Harbour Hotel but, in the mood he was in, I really didn't want to leave Ben on his own. I was surprised Jools hadn't come back yet, and then I started worrying about her.

I knew it. My evening was going to be a disaster. I rang my daughter's mobile.

She answered – thank God.

'Just wondering where you were . . .'

'Still at Fourteen Seacrest Avenue. And, Mum, you won't believe it – I've just found Cedric's laptop!'

FOURTEEN

I tried not to sound too manic in my urging of Jools to get back as soon as possible. 'You may have forgotten I'm going out for dinner.'

'Oh yes. But surely Ben'll be . . .?' Then, remembering family history, she said, 'I'll be right back.' It was a long time since I'd heard my daughter show such sensitivity.

Jools was back before half past seven, triumphantly brandishing the laptop. She stopped in the hall and took in my appearance. 'Gosh, Mum, you scrub up a treat when you make the effort.'

'Thank you, Jools,' I said drily.

'Anyway,' she continued, bouncy with excitement, 'ask me how I found the laptop.'

'I haven't really got time for guessing games.'

'No, listen. I was really proud of myself.' It was the tone of reproof she'd used when I didn't instantly drop what I was doing to admire the painting she'd brought back from primary school.

I looked at my watch. 'All right. How did you find it?'

'I thought myself into Cedric Waites's mind. I thought, if I was a reclusive widower in my late seventies and I had a laptop I wanted to keep hidden, where would I put it?'

'And . . .?' I prompted.

'And . . . I thought it's got to be somewhere nobody would think of looking. Though, actually, if you don't let anyone into your house, why would you bother hiding a laptop, anyway?'

From my knowledge of hoarders, I could have given her lots of explanations for that, but not right then. 'Look, Jools, I have got to go and—'

'Well, as I say, I got inside Cedric Waites's mind and I thought—'

At that moment, we were interrupted by the landline ringing.

I answered it. 'Oh, hello, Ellen darling.' It was my mother. All that I needed.

'Hello, Fleur.'

'Darling, I've been so worried about you.'

'Worried about me?'

'You haven't rung me for so long. And I've been desperately worried about Jools too. Have you heard anything from my bestie?'

God, she certainly knew the words to rile me.

'Jools?' I said, for a moment uncertain whether to say I hadn't seen her or to own up.

Then, to my amazement, my daughter took the phone from me. Oh no, I thought. I can't stand hearing Jools going into the high-camp, brittle persona she always assumes when talking to her grandmother.

But no. My daughter spoke firmly into the receiver. 'Fleur, this is Jools speaking. As you can hear, I'm absolutely fine. But Mum and I have got a lot of stuff to sort out. So, we need some time on our own, without you interfering. One of us'll call you in a couple of days.'

And she put the phone down. I gazed at her in astonishment and admiration. Jools had just said what I had been longing to say to my mother for around fifty years.

But I hadn't got time to pass comment. 'Look, I really must go. And . . . keep an eye on Ben.'

'Will do. Actually, I'll see if he has any ideas for getting round the password on Cedric's laptop.'

'Good idea. Must dash. And, look,' I continued awkwardly, 'if I'm back late, don't worry.'

'Dirty stop-out,' said Jools.

Which didn't help.

Tim Goodrich had deliberately placed his room key on the table next to his side plate. An obvious symbolic gesture perhaps, but it wasn't a symbolism I objected to. When something feels right, it feels right.

Given the misgivings I had had coming up to the dinner, in the event it was all very relaxed. I remember the terrible anxiety Oliver used to suffer from before public occasions. For days, even weeks before, he would be imagining all of the ghastly things that could go wrong, never making the big assumption that in fact they might be all right. And, of course, they always

were. Oliver was charming and relaxed and funny and no one
would imagine the paroxysms of doubt he had suffered in the
run-up. I think depressives are kind of shielded in a way. Nothing
reality can offer is as bad as their worst imaginings. In a genuine
crisis they can be extremely effective.

It always makes me think of that line of Julius Caesar's in
Shakespeare's play: 'Cowards die many times before their death;
the valiant never taste of death but once.' Strange to apply that
quote to depressives, but for me it makes sense.

Strange too, it might be thought, to be thinking of Oliver in
my current situation. But that too seemed to make sense. I had
no feeling of betraying him. Instead, I felt a kind of liberation.
I was embarking on a new chapter of my life, and I felt, bizarrely,
that I was doing so with my late husband's full approval.

It was a long time since I'd drunk a gin and tonic, but when
Tim suggested we start with one, it felt like a good idea. Pink
gin he went for, something I had rarely tasted (I think only once,
that time with Jools). Good, though. And, again, he ordered
Malbec to go with the meal.

I chose, to start with, Whipped Goat's Curd (with beets,
pear and bitter leaf salad) and, as a main course, Halibut Fillet
(with seaweed butter, Atlantic prawns, mussels and leeks). Red
wine with fish again, yummy. Tim went for the Moules
Marinière starter, followed by Slow Cooked Lamb Shoulder
(with dauphinois potatoes, seasonal greens and cider jus, to
complete all the description).

We didn't initially talk about it, but we both knew how
the evening was destined to end up. And both felt relaxed and
happy about that. Like I just said, when something feels right,
it feels right.

We had plenty else to talk about, anyway. I was intrigued to
know how Roy and Michelle had taken the news that they were
excluded from Cedric's will.

Tim chuckled. 'Total amazement, I would say just about covers
it. And, in Michelle's case, total fury. She even had the nerve to
say, "after all we've done for him!" She's one very unhappy lady.
It turns out – you know she's some kind of academic?'

'Yes. Women's Studies, wasn't it?'

'Exactly. Which is a minefield at the moment, with all the

trans issues and debates about that ever-expanding acronym, LGBT. I see a lot of it happening in Oxford, though – thank God – it hasn't actually arisen in the world of serotonin research. It could, though, it could at any minute. All it needs is for someone to use an inappropriate pronoun discussing the difference in effects of antidepressants on men and women and – wow! World War Three starts.

'Anyway, it seems that Michelle Waites's views on these matters have proved unpopular with her university authorities, unpopular to the point of her losing her job. Some very nasty goings-on at Senior Common Room level. Lots on social media too, a real Twitter-storm. Apparently there's some senior academic – another woman inevitably – who's really got her claws out for Michelle. If you have a couple of hours to spare, you could ask Michelle about it. Should you fancy hearing some choice language, ask her about the authoritarian vegan, named Bobbi, who has elbowed her out of her job. Anyway, I get the impression Michelle was hoping their inheritance from Cedric would fill the gap caused by her lack of income.'

'Do you think they're genuinely hard up?'

Tim shrugged. 'No idea. I can't think – unless they have secret vices I know not of – that their outgoings are very high. They don't have children . . . as Michelle kept telling me. They don't have children because they don't think it's responsible to bring more people into the world. They have not had children for the good of the planet . . . though I think – if any children they had turned out like Michelle – they're doing it for the good of humankind.'

I grinned. It was relaxing to be with someone who shared my rather acid sense of humour.

'And how did they react to the news that you were a beneficiary?'

'Frank disbelief, initially. Which, I must say, was rather how I responded when I first read the will. I mean, I liked the pair of them. Was probably closer to Flick than I was to Cedric, but not kind of beneficiary-of-a-will close. The bequest seemed very unlikely to me. And even more unlikely to Michelle. She virtually accused me of forging the will.'

'How did she think you might have done that?'

'Oh, God knows. She wasn't at her most rational. And she refused to believe that I hadn't seen a copy of it until this week. She said, as executor, I must have done. And then she virtually accused me of murdering Cedric to speed up my inheritance.'

'Did Roy contribute anything to this conversation?'

'A lot of "Yes, love"s and "You're absolutely right, love"s.' He grinned. 'What were you expecting?'

'Exactly that. So, are the pair of them still in Chichester? Wasn't there some talk of the funeral being next week?'

'Talk, yes. But it won't be happening for a while. The police still haven't released the body.'

'Which would imply their investigation is still ongoing.'

'I guess so.'

'Incidentally,' I went on, 'I did hear this afternoon from your . . . what's the word . . .? "Co-inheritor"?'

'Vi Spelling?'

'Yes.'

'I haven't met her yet. Well, I saw her in Seacrest Avenue, when she talked to you . . . you know, that time we met at Cedric's place with Roy and Michelle.'

'I remember.'

'And I've talked to her on the phone. In my role as executor, you know, to tell her about her good fortune. Why did she ring you?'

'Initially, she wanted to know if I too was a beneficiary of the will.'

'Why should she think that?'

'Because she was. Because you were too, come to that. People who weren't very close to Cedric, but who had helped him since Flick's death. I suppose I just about fitted into that category.'

'Hm.'

'Anyway, I invited her round for tea.'

'Oh? And did you get any clearer impression of the relationship she had with Cedric?'

'Not really. I think, like most of their acquaintances, she knew Flick better than she knew him.'

Tim looked thoughtful. 'So, Vi, like me, was a fairly random choice of beneficiary?'

'Seems that way.'

'Which makes it even clearer that, when Cedric drew up his will, his only aim was to antagonize Roy and Michelle.'

'I can't see any other explanation.'

'No.' He tapped his chin and took another sip of Malbec. 'I wonder what they'd done to make him so angry?'

I too resorted to the Malbec. It was delicious, perfect with my halibut. We seemed to be making our way down the bottle quite speedily. Noticing this, Tim waved at the waitress for a replacement. I didn't mind. I was feeling no pain.

In spite of the increasingly promising romantic situation I found myself in, I was still intrigued by the circumstances of Cedric's death. 'One thing Vi said that interested me was how disorganized Cedric was about his food. He just stuffed the freezer with everything he bought or was given, and there was no system in the order in which he ate the various meals.'

'Which means that the container with the fatal dose of oleander in it could have been there for some time?'

'Exactly. I'm also still intrigued by the way he kept defrosting the freezer. Though he let other electrical devices quietly expire, he made sure that that kept working.'

'Self-preservation?'

I smiled wryly. 'If that was the intention, it didn't work, did it?'

'No.'

'So, Ellen, if we were playing amateur detectives, who would be our suspects, the ones who could have delivered a poisoned container of food and waited for the Russian Roulette moment when Cedric selected that particular one to have for his supper?'

'Well, if we exclude crazed supermarket employees who get their kicks from randomly injecting poison into the products on their frozen food shelves . . .'

Tim chuckled. 'Let's exclude them . . . for the time being.'

'Fine. Way back, just after Flick's death, Michelle said she prepared some meals for him, "stocked the freezer" with them. But we're talking eight years ago. I would have thought he'd have eaten those before he got into his regular Ocado ordering. Sadly, I don't think we can pin this one on Michelle.'

'What a pity,' said Tim. 'I like to think the best of most people. For Michelle Waites, I'm prepared to make an exception.'

I liked the way that his thinking so exactly matched my own.
'OK, Tim, putting her to one side . . .'

'With reluctance.'

'With reluctance, certainly. The other person we know prepared
meals for Cedric was Vi Spelling.'

'Yes. Who was also a beneficiary of his will. Which means
she had means and motive. So, if this were a Golden Age
whodunit . . .'

'But it isn't, Tim.'

'No.'

'Vi didn't know about her inheritance. Can you really see her
in the role of murderer?'

Ruefully, Tim shook his head. 'Next suspect?'

'Me.'

'You?'

'I put meals in containers for Cedric. In the last few months,
he'd eaten quite a lot of my cooking.'

'And what might your motive be, Ellen?'

'Mentally unhinged?' I offered.

'No!' said Tim forcefully. 'I refuse to believe that someone I
care for so much would be capable of such an appalling crime.'

Though said with irony, it was the first time he had expressed
his feelings for me so directly. I didn't mind.

'What about the avid recycler you mentioned? Dodd, was it?'

'Dodge. He did prepare some meals for Cedric, it's true.'

'And what sort of cooking does he do?'

'Vegetarian. Often stuff he's foraged. He uses lots of leaves
and herbs. And he grows lots of his own stuff.'

'Including oleander? Does he grow oleander?'

I didn't want to admit the truth, but Tim moved straight on to
his next question. 'And you tell me this Dodge has done a runner?'

'Yes,' I agreed wretchedly.

Tim pursed his lips. 'Doesn't look good.'

'No,' I admitted. 'But if the food he gave to Cedric was
poisoned, Dodge wouldn't have done it deliberately. It would
have been an accident.'

'If it was an accident, why would he have run away? Surely,
he could have told the police?'

I hadn't got the energy to describe Dodge's paranoia about

the police. This turn in the conversation seemed to have cast a pall over the evening. I felt low, embarrassed by my former expectations.

But Tim's mood didn't seem to be affected. He said, with a shy smile, 'One thing I'd like to get straight, Ellen . . .'

'Hm?'

'To avoid awkwardness later . . .'

'OK.'

'If, at the end of the meal, I were to suggest you might join me for a nightcap in my room . . .' I didn't say anything '. . . would you go all offended and MeToo on me?'

I looked him straight in the eyes. They were brown, vulnerable, pleading. I said, 'No, I wouldn't go all offended and MeToo on you. I would think it was a very attractive idea.'

'Good,' he said. 'I'm glad we've got that out of the way.' The evident relief in his manner made me aware of the tension he had felt before broaching the subject. The elephant in the room, whose presence had been evident to both of us all evening. I felt even more warmth towards him.

From then on, we just chatted. Light chit-chat, likes and dislikes; nothing contentious, nothing that mattered. Just enjoyable talking.

Tim said we should have a nightcap in the restaurant before the one we had upstairs and he ordered Armagnac. I had drunk much more than I usually did that evening, but I felt totally in control of myself. I knew exactly what I was doing. And I welcomed what was about to happen.

Then my mobile buzzed. It was a text. From Jools.

'Sorry, Mum. You've got to come back. It's Ben.'

FIFTEEN

There was a noose hanging down from the banisters. Made from that bright blue nylon rope that gets washed up on seashores. The kind that Dodge uses for making chair seats.

I'd run all the way from the hotel. I couldn't wait around for a cab, difficult to get at that time in the centre of Chichester, anyway. When I burst into the hall, Jools was sitting at the bottom of the stairs, tears were pouring down her face.

'Where is he?' I demanded.

'In his bedroom.'

At least not in hospital. But that reassurance was swept away by the thought that she might have moved his body there. I rushed past her up the stairs and threw myself against Ben's door. It opened easily.

He lay on the bed, with a whisky bottle in his hand. He looked up at me. 'Sorry, Ma,' he said.

'Why, Ben? Why?'

'Sorry. Just the tension. I couldn't stand it. I couldn't stand being me any more, Ma.'

'Look, I know what it's about, Ben.'

'Do you, Ma? Do you really?'

'It's not that important, you've got to understand. All right, so you didn't win an award in some animation festival. The TOCA Film Festival in Turin? What does that even mean? It doesn't mean your *Riq and Raq* film is rubbish. It doesn't mean you're rubbish. It just . . . Oh, Ben . . .'

And now I couldn't stop the tears pouring down my face.

After a long silence, Ben said, 'But I didn't lose, Ma. *Riq and Raq* won.'

I remembered, with Oliver, it had been the same. When he'd achieved something, when the tension broke, the depression came flooding in. Like when we'd been through a really bad patch financially, then suddenly he got a twenty grand commission for a commercial animation. He went down for three months after that.

I said to Ben, there in his bedroom. 'The noose? Would you have used it?'

'Oh yes, Ma,' he replied.

I sent a text to Tim Goodrich. 'Sorry. Family crisis. Will explain.' And then I dared to put: 'Love, Ellen.'

But could I explain? And would he understand my explanation? Or would he just think he'd wasted an evening with a gauche, post-menopausal woman who'd led him along and lost her nerve at the last minute?

He texted back straight away. 'No worries. Get back to me when things are sorted. X T.' Which could have meant anything. And the worries I had at that moment definitely took precedence over my so-called romantic life.

The means by which it was achieved is not one recommended in most manuals of parenting, but the night that followed was the best family time the three of us had shared since Oliver's death. And the catalyst, I'm afraid, was alcohol.

Waiting in panic for the results of the TOCA Award from Turin, Ben had already made his way down most of a bottle of whisky. Jools favoured pink gin, of which she seemed to have a ready supply. And I, full of Tim's largesse at the Chichester Harbour Hotel, joined Ben topping up on the whisky.

The first thing I insisted he did was to take down the noose. Then Jools said it should be ceremoniously burnt in the back garden. I found some white spirit I'd used when I last did any decorating, and we doused the rope in that. Then we laid the noose on a paved area and Ben – Jools demanded it should be Ben – put a match to it.

I hadn't seen nylon rope burn before. It wasn't what I expected. The blue strands melted and bubbled, as the rope coiled in on itself like some sci-fi serpent. A whitish smoke played around it and there was a smell of fish in the air.

And as it burned, my two children – and 'children' was the appropriate word on this occasion – started to do a war dance around the burning rope, whooping, hollering and chanting in some made-up language of their own. I had seen them do this before, but not for nearly twenty years. And, back then, Oliver joined in too. I never did. I wasn't disapproving. I just watched them, as I did again that Saturday night, in admiring astonishment.

The irrelevant thought came to me that what they were doing, imitating some primitive tribal ritual, would now be condemned as 'cultural appropriation'. But that didn't worry me. Nor did what the neighbours thought. Actually, the neighbours might have objected to the noise, but that would have been all. Cultural appropriation is not a major concern to the good burghers of Chichester.

When the last wisp of white smoke had dissolved into the darkness, we continued our drinking in the sitting room. We continued our talking too.

A lot came out. Perhaps inevitably, it was all about Oliver. And not before time.

At first Jools talked most. I'd heard some of it in the previous few days, since I'd rescued her from Herne Hill. But the pink gin opened her out in ways I could never have expected.

And no, I didn't emerge unscathed from her cataract of commentary. She actually said out loud that she thought I'd always favoured Ben. It wasn't something I'd really worried about before. My son was so like his father that I could never be unaware of his vulnerability and so yes, maybe his sister had suffered as a result. But Jools had made herself so unapproachable, getting through had always been a problem.

The other significant revelation she made was the guilt she felt for Oliver's death. When she matured into her teens, it was inevitable that the cuddly bond he'd had with his infant Juliet should change to something less intimate. As she grew more morose and bolshie, she had shrugged off his hugs and deliberately not laughed at his jokes (even though she still thought they were funny). In other words, she had behaved like any other teenage girl but, in the light of her father's suicide, she had started to believe that it had been caused by her behaviour. It was then that she had begun to shut herself off from unwelcome emotions.

By the time Jools handed the baton of criticism over to Ben,

they were both very drunk. Mind you, so was I, so I'm not about
to get into a pot-and-kettle routine. And Ben too had some gripes
about the way I'd looked after him. Phrases like 'being over-
protective' and 'not letting me lead a life of my own' swirled
around in his denunciation. I tried just to take it all, not to let it
get to me. In our drunken state, there was no point in starting
arguments. See how much of it any of us remembered in the
morning.

In characteristic style, Ben's mood had suddenly flipped. The
release of tension over the TOCA Award, whose first effect had
been to turn him suicidal, was replaced by a giggly excitement
about the fact that he had won. Ben Curtis's *Riq and Raq* film
had actually won a prize at an Animation Festival in Turin! It
was an accolade to be put on his professional CV, one that could
never be taken away from him.

And sure, he didn't know how prestigious the Turin Festival
was, where it ranked in the grown-up animation world he so
wanted to join, but it was a start. His profile would grow. He
might be asked to show *Riq and Raq* at other animation festivals.
It might lead to offers of work, even the Holy Grail of getting
an agent.

Ben Curtis might have failed to complete a degree course – I
hadn't realized until then how much that failure rankled with
him – but he had won a TOCA Award at the Turin Animation
Festival!

By now, he was getting rambling and repetitive. His eyes kept
closing and he lay full-length on the sofa. Jools had been asleep
for some twenty minutes, curled up in an armchair like she had
when she was three. I got up to turn the sitting-room lights off,
leaving the door ajar to let in a glow from the hall. Then I curled
up in my armchair and let my eyes droop closed.

We felt more like a family than we had for nearly ten years.

And Tim Goodrich belonged to another world.

SIXTEEN

The light coming through the cracks in the curtains woke me. It wasn't seven yet. I'm sensitive to light and my head was particularly sensitive to that morning's light. It bored into my eyeballs with all the delicacy of a corkscrew.

Jools was still curled up like a woodlouse in her armchair, apparently not having moved all night. Ben was draped on his back over the sofa with one arm drooping on to the floor, rather in the manner of *The Death of Chatterton*. It was an unsettling comparison. The young poet in the painting had just killed himself with arsenic. I was reminded of the night before, not the drunken confessionals, but the image which had greeted me when I entered the house. The blue nylon noose tied to the banisters. I shuddered.

The sitting room smelled of adolescence.

Hot, strong coffee was called for. Next, out of the night-before's glad rags for a hot, strong shower. After that, jeans and a baggy T-shirt. Then work out what to do with our Sunday.

That thought reminded me of one thing the day would not contain – an encounter with Fleur. Even through my hangover, I couldn't repress a feeling of glee when I remembered what my daughter had said to my mother.

I decided that, when my children woke, we would all have a large, kill-or-cure fry-up brunch.

My offspring came back to life slowly that Sunday morning. Just like when they were adolescents. With, of course, the added burden of thumping hangovers. Jools was grumpy and monosyllabic. Also, in pain. She'd somehow slept in a position that put pressure on her recently stitched nose. I wondered how soon she'd be able to get that appointment with the surgeon at St Richard's.

She shuffled off bad-temperedly to shower and put some clothes on.

I had to wait longer for Ben. I was going through sensations that I hadn't experienced since the unmourned 'ladette' days of my early twenties. Not to put too fine a point on it, I desperately wanted another drink. To dilute the pain in my head. The buzz of more alcohol. It was a very long time since I'd felt that urgency. God, what a sedate, middle-aged woman I had become.

I resisted the temptation and made more coffee.

As I drank it, an unwelcome thought came into my head. About Ben and the timing of his suicidal gesture the night before. Although I had kept my relationship with Tim very low-key, hardly mentioned it, in fact, had my son intuited that something was going on? Had the thought of a new man in his mother's life made him jealous?

Oh God, I'd got quite enough on my plate without having to deal with an Oedipus Complex.

But, as I had that thought, I wondered whether I was being paranoid about Ben. And whether part of my reaction to the wrecking of the previous evening's plans had been relief.

When Ben finally emerged from the sitting room, he looked terrible. His breath smelt like a blocked drain in a distillery. And he was very surly.

Which was good. 'Surly' may be unpleasant to live with, but it isn't 'depressed'. I'd been around Oliver enough to know the difference.

As soon as he left the sitting room, I opened the windows to fumigate the space. Ran the vacuum over the carpet. And plumped up the sofa cushions where Ben had been lying. (Why is the concept of plumping up cushions so alien to men?)

Another entry in my Bad Parenting Guide: A Hair of the Dog really helps a hangover.

When I finally got my green-faced son and daughter round the kitchen table, before I even embarked on the frying, I opened a bottle of Merlot. I'm afraid I took an immediate slurp from my glass and felt vindicated when Ben and Jools did the same. And again I had the unworthy thought: Thank God Fleur isn't here.

As I started cooking, something happened which again reminded me of my boozy early twenties. With the hydration of

more alcohol, we all quickly got drunk again. Some of the hilarity
of the previous evening returned.

Jools started fantasizing about how her botched nose-job would
eventually turn out. Obviously, this was a potential worrying
conjecture but at that moment it seemed hysterical to her.

And Ben, tension draining from him with each swallow of
wine, started to express his dreams for the effect his TOCA Award
might have on his career. He was quite funny about that too. Got
into a great routine about the actors he'd like to voice his animated
characters – and the ones he'd particularly like to be in the
recording studio with. Quite a revelation for a mother to hear
about her son's taste in women.

Though I say it myself, I do do a good fry-up. I'm particularly proud of the oily crunchiness I get into my fried bread.
And I always include black pudding. Some kids don't like it,
particularly once they've heard it called 'blood sausage', but it
had been part of our family diet for so long that Ben and Jools
absolutely love it.

When the hilarity died down, we all started to behave more
soberly. I guess we'd reached the 'maintenance dose' level which
keeps serious alcoholics functioning. And the conversation moved
on to other subjects.

Particularly Dodge.

Ben had been in such a bad state the day before that we hadn't
really had a chance to debrief about our unsuccessful mission to
Portsmouth. But as we talked around the kitchen table, I realized
I'd have to tell Ben and Jools more about Dodge's disappearance
than I might have wanted to. Explaining why he'd done a runner
meant mentioning his distrust of the police. Then Ben wanted to
know why the police were involved, which meant I had to tell
them about the suspicions surrounding Cedric Waites's death. It
was more information than I really liked to disclose about my
work.

But what I told them seemed to get Ben and Jools excited.
They responded to the unsolved crime element in the situation.
Jools revealed to me that she'd 'always loved whodunits', some-
thing which, to my shame, I had not been aware of. Mind you,
getting any insight about interests and feelings from the teenage
Jools had always made marathons look like strolls in the park.

Ben was equally enthused, particularly interested in the cause of Cedric's death. I found myself going through the list of people who might have supplied the poisoned meal, just as I had with Tim the evening before.

'Dodge does have pots of oleander around the place,' he observed. 'He's shown them to me. Trying to get me as obsessed with all his foraging and herbal remedies as he is.' He smiled wryly. 'Unsuccessfully. I'm afraid I can't get very excited about that stuff.'

'No,' said Jools, 'but if he has got plants like oleander around and he's doing all this vegetarian cooking, then surely there's a chance that the poison got into the food by mistake?'

'I have considered that possibility.' I sighed. 'I'm really starting to get quite worried about Dodge.'

'He's got a phone, has he?' asked Jools.

'Oh yes. But you can't make someone pick up, can you? I've tried a good few times, but I reckon, as soon as he saw it was me, he decided not to answer. And, God knows, if he has gone feral and is living out in the wild somewhere, will he even be able to charge a mobile?'

'I think he'll do his best to,' said Ben.

'Why do you say that?'

'In case of emergency calls from . . . you know, the people he helps . . . People like Pat. Dodge is their lifeline.'

Ben had to explain to his sister about the missing man's work with drug charities. Jools looked thoughtful for a moment, then said, 'I think we're in a position which occurs quite often in the crime fiction I enjoy reading.'

'Oh yes?' I said. 'And what position is that?'

'It's the one where the only way of stopping someone being the police's prime suspect is by proving that they didn't commit the crime. And the only way of achieving that is by finding out who actually did do it.'

'Thank you very much, Jools,' I said wearily. 'That's a real help.'

But I had a nasty feeling she was right.

And I felt even more stupid for having destroyed the one piece of evidence which might have revealed the perpetrator.

* * *

I had noticed, while we were eating, Ben's mobile kept pinging. What he saw on the screen annoyed him and he didn't respond to any of the attempted contacts. After a while he switched the phone off and put it firmly in his pocket.

I couldn't help wondering whether the calls or texts were from Pippa. Her name had not been mentioned since Ben had lost his temper and shouted at me. Did she even know that he had won the TOCA Award she had kept 'going on about'?

I didn't dare indulge my fantasy that the split between them might be permanent. Oh dear, was I making my own contribution to the Oedipus scenario?

When we had finished the brunch and opened a second bottle of Merlot, we took our calorie-stuffed bodies back to the sitting room, slumping into the same chairs we had only vacated a few hours earlier. Ben's subsidence on to the sofa cushions instantly undid my efforts at plumping them. He had the wine with him and kept topping up his glass. Jools and I didn't feel the immediate need for more.

A not-unpleasant torpor settled over us. I reflected how bizarre it was that a family rapprochement had been engineered by a botched nose job and an attempted suicide. Life has never been predictable.

We might well have all drifted back to sleep again if Jools hadn't suddenly shouted, 'The laptop!'

'What?'

'Cedric's laptop! I'd completely forgotten, but we may have in the house the evidence that will solve everything!'

'Oh yes,' I said. 'By the way, you never did tell me where you found it.'

'I didn't.' Jools grinned. Somehow, with the dressing still covering her nose, it made her look comical. 'Well, like I said, I tried to think inside Cedric's mind.'

I nodded approval. That's my girl.

'And I thought . . . Why does a man who never lets anyone inside his home bother about hiding his laptop . . . particularly when, as you told me, he makes no attempt to hide a briefcase containing a large amount of money?

'And that made me think that perhaps the need to keep his

laptop hidden pre-dated his wife's death – and that it was her he wanted to hide it from.'

I liked the way my daughter's mind was working, but her theory didn't seem to fit the facts. Everyone who knew them seemed to have regarded the Waiteses' marriage as perfect. Yes, Flick was more outgoing than her husband, but that was just how the relationship worked. Surely he wouldn't need to have secrets from such a wife?

On the other hand, past experiences – and particularly instances I have encountered in my SpaceWoman work – tell me that there are secrets in every marriage. And no outsider can ever really know what's going on inside. I waited while Jools developed her theory.

'So, I thought . . . where would Cedric Waites have put something he didn't want his wife to find? And I remembered you telling me that Flick . . . was that her name?' I nodded '. . . wasn't interested in books. And I found at the bottom of Cedric's bookcase, there was a very shallow drawer that pulled out. You'd never notice unless you were looking for it. And in that drawer,' she concluded with quiet satisfaction, 'was the laptop.'

'Well done, Jools,' I said.

Ben clapped his hands twice and said, in a crusty colonel voice, 'Excellent sleuthing, Holmes.'

Jools grinned, said, 'I'll get it,' and rushed up to her bedroom.

It wasn't the latest model of laptop but it wasn't laughably old-fashioned either. Probably bought within the last ten years. So he'd had it while Flick was still alive.

The battery had been completely dead but fortunately Jools had found a charging cable in the hidden drawer. She put the laptop on a low table in the sitting room and switched it on.

The screen came to life but, needless to say, a password was needed to access any data.

'Any bright ideas?' Jools asked Ben, who was peering over her shoulder at the screen.

'Oh yes.' Her brother grinned. '"Password-protected" is a relative term these days. I reckon the laptop has yet to be invented that I can't get into.'

'I know a few ways of doing it too,' said Jools, with a matching grin.

There was a complicity between them, born of their shared technological knowledge. I felt excluded, a Luddite, a dinosaur.

'Be simplest,' said Ben, 'if I get my laptop. I can do it from there.'

'Just a minute,' I said. 'Can we just try it the old-fashioned way?'

They exchanged puzzled glances. 'What "old-fashioned way"?'

'Guessing the right password.'

The looks they exchanged now were frankly incredulous, unable to believe that there was anyone left in the world who was so naïve.

'Try putting in "Flick",' I said to Jools.

Wearily, humouring me, she did as instructed. And there was no disguising the glee on her face when the laptop refused to yield up its secrets.

'Try "Flick1",' I said.

More elaborate eye-rolling as she did that. Impudent glee when that too failed.

'"Flick1-2",' I said firmly.

Jools keyed it in. The laptop unlocked.

I got treated to one of Ben's ironic double-hand claps. 'Well done, Ma. Intuitive or what?'

I was impervious to being sent up by my own flesh and blood. Too interested in what the laptop's contents might reveal about the secret life of Cedric Waites.

We had no trouble getting into his email account. Hotmail. Old-fashioned. That figured.

He clearly didn't use email much and, of course, he'd only had the router reconnected relatively recently. There were no exchanges with Roy and Michelle. Ocado shopping orders. And intermittent correspondence about potential book purchases with Augustus Mintzen. That seemed to be it. Except for junk mail, of course, some of which infiltrated his Inbox.

The laptop didn't provide the instant revelations I'd been hoping for.

Still, maybe there'd be something in his Word documents.

But I was prevented from further investigation by my landline ringing.

'Hello?'

'Is that you, Ellen dear? It's Vi Spelling.'

'Oh, nice to hear you.'

I was about to ask, politely of course, what she wanted, but the old woman needed no prompt.

'You remember. Ellen, when I come to your place yesterday . . .?' God, was it only yesterday? Several lifetimes seemed to have passed in the interim.

'Yes.'

'. . . you said if I remembered seeing anyone else going to Cedric's house, I should tell you.'

'Mm.'

'Well, it come back to me. Someone did come round, months back it was, before Christmas, I think. I'd forgotten all about it, but it was a day when I was taking a prepared meal round for Cedric . . . and you know, he'd left a fiver for me on the back doorstep, like I said. And when I come round the front of the house, there's this woman knocking on the front door. And I tell her she's wasting her time, Cedric doesn't open his door to anyone, and she asks me why, has he got hoarding problems? I say yes, he has, and she says maybe she could help him. And I say he won't take help from anyone, not if it involves letting them into his house.

'Anyway, she's quite persistent and says I should tell Cedric she called. And she gave me her business card, so's he could get in touch. "Make sure you tell him," she said. "I'm sure I can help sort out his problems."'

'And did you tell him?'

'Yes, of course I did. And just like I'd told her he would, Cedric said he wasn't interested. Didn't want to know about it.'

'And do you still have the business card?' I asked tentatively.

'Yes, I kept it.'

Feeling pretty certain that I knew the answer, I asked what the woman's name was.

And, sure enough, Vi Spelling said that the company was called BrightHome and the woman's name was Rosemary Findlay.

I felt even more as if she was stalking me.

SEVENTEEN

When I got on to the BrightHome website, I was struck once again by how like the SpaceWoman one it was. Offering the same services, the same positive testimonials, the same smiling photograph of the boss.

Except my reaction to the photograph was different this time. Since my last viewing, I had seen its subject. Not talked to, just seen. Seen leaving a second-hand bookshop in Petworth. The woman who'd looked vaguely familiar had quite definitely been Rosemary Findlay.

I riffled through some papers which had accumulated on the hall table. (For someone whose job is decluttering, I can sometimes be blithely oblivious to the clutter which accumulates in my own home.) And I found what I was looking for. The catalogue which Augustus Mintzen had thrust on me when I was leaving his shop some ten days before.

I read through the contents with some interest. And then rang Allegra Cramond. She didn't pick up, so I left a message.

Ben and Jools were both in bed by ten that Sunday evening. They had a lot of booze to sleep off. I hadn't had any more since the end of the brunch and, after a fairly headachey afternoon, I now felt back on an even keel. And I had a lot to think about.

Some of it was positive, like the trail I hoped I had started with Allegra. Other thoughts were less welcome. Alcohol may postpone problems, it never solves them. And the fact remained that, though the last twenty-four hours had passed in a giggly haze, I still had two children with serious problems.

Jools's London world had fallen apart, and we didn't know whether her dealings with unregulated Hungarian surgeons would leave her permanently scarred. And on the Saturday evening Ben, though he was characteristically jokey about it afterwards, had really contemplated suicide.

Neither could be left on their own for any length of time.

Then, at some point, bridges would have to be rebuilt with Fleur.

I was also feeling a level of guilt about Tim Goodrich. Recent shocks prevented me from defining the current nature of our relationship (if indeed we had one), but I knew that the attraction between us had been genuine. And I think mutual.

I dared to ring his mobile number. He didn't pick up. I didn't blame him.

No fixed SpaceWoman appointments scheduled for the Monday but there were things I wanted to do. One was to visit Mim Galbraith and pick her brains about the time Rosemary Findlay had spent with her. And there was still the clearance job at 14 Seacrest Avenue.

I almost felt I could trust Jools to continue there on her own. Or we could get on with it together. But that would leave Ben on his own. And I desperately didn't want to leave Ben on his own. As I made my breakfast coffee, I was no nearer to knowing how to manage the day.

But, serendipitously, my children were ahead of me. Sometime the previous evening or that morning they had talked and devised a plan which answered all my immediate needs.

Both of them were surprisingly together and business-like. With the enviable bounce-back of youth, neither seemed still to be affected by the prodigious amounts of alcohol they'd consumed over the weekend.

'I'd been thinking, Ma,' said Ben, 'about Dodge.'

'Yes, of course. Me too.' My worries about him had just moved further back in the queue.

'I know Pat had no ideas where he might be, but there are a few other of his Portsmouth contacts who might be worth talking to.'

'Anything that gives us a chance of finding him, obviously we must try it.'

'I thought what Jools and I would do is get the train to Portsmouth.'

'I'd happily drive you, Ben.'

'No,' said Jools, rather too quickly.

'Better if we go by train.' Ben explained, 'Then, when we've talked to some people, I can bring Dodge's van back. I've got a spare pair of keys.'

'All right.'

'And, Ma, if we need to go off somewhere to find Dodge, we'll have transport.'

'Good idea.'

'Also,' said Jools, perhaps unnecessarily, 'it'll be better if you're not there when we talk to the druggies.'

'What?'

'Well, someone of your age might inhibit them. You know, too much of a do-gooding authority figure.'

Nice to know how one's children see one, isn't it?

But I was very pleased by Ben and Jools's suggestion. If the two of them were together, I could relax a bit. And it might reinforce the bonding between them that I had observed develop in the last forty-eight hours. Also, I was as desperate as they were for Dodge to be found.

So, this was delegation, something that hadn't really happened before in the SpaceWoman world. And my next encounter might lead to more delegation.

Allegra had rung back on the dot of nine. I reckoned that, in her highly organized world, everything happened on the dot. And, for her, nine in the morning was a reasonable hour to ring anyone.

We agreed to meet in Buon Caffè, a non-chain Chichester coffee shop run by a lovely guy called Giovanni. I go there often enough for him to start preparing a flat white as soon as he sees me. Though I arrived, as per arrangement, 'on the dot' of ten thirty, Allegra Cramond was already there. She downed her double espresso in one and rose to greet me.

'Sorry, habit I got into when I lived in Italy,' she said. 'You don't sip coffee in Italy. You gulp it down, preferably while it's still hot enough to scorch your oesophagus.'

She shook me firmly by the hand. Allegra Cramond wasn't a huggy-kissy sort of woman. In her various Foreign Office postings, I think she'd found a firm handshake more effective.

'Anyway, give me the dirt,' she said, when we were both sitting down.

I had taken my laptop with me and opened up the BrightHome

website. It was familiar to Allegra. That was how she had made
contact with Rosemary Findlay in the first place.

Then I showed her the relevant entry in Augustus Mintzen's
catalogue. She was as shocked as I had been.

'God! So she's been screwing over Mim Galbraith.'

'That's the way it looks.'

'I'll see she pays for this. In a court of law.'

'You'll have to get proof.'

'I'll get proof,' said Allegra Cramond, in the gung-ho manner
by which the British Empire had been built (before everyone
came to realize that it shouldn't have been built in the first place).
'Do you want to be involved when I confront them?'

'You bet I do!'

When I left Buon Caffè I was tempted to ring Tim Goodrich
again. But no, I'd left him a message on the Sunday evening. The
ball was in his court. And if he chose to leave it there, in
the dust against the netting with all the other discarded balls,
I had only myself to blame. Or Ben to blame, possibly. But I
wasn't in the habit of blaming Ben.

I could go back to 14 Seacrest Avenue. There was still plenty
to do there.

But the call of Cedric's laptop was stronger.

I don't know what I was expecting to have found. There didn't
seem to be any work stuff on file, but that was hardly surprising.
It was a long time since he'd retired. A solicitor in the charity
sector, I recalled. No doubt he'd had a work computer then.
Anyway, he and Flick's retirement plans, so soon to be destroyed,
had been to travel the world. A complete change of direction
from their working lives. There was no reason for him to have
kept anything from his days of employment.

I did find a Word directory called 'Charity' but all he seemed
to have filed there were emails requesting funds or saying how
effective legacies could be, 'continuing to help people once you
can no longer help them in person'. I wondered if Cedric had
left anything to charity in his will. A possible reason to ring his
executor to find out? I put the thought from my mind.

He had a directory entitled 'Books', which recorded details

of his collection, wish-lists and contacts. Records of his dealings with Augustus Mintzen. But, again, nothing unexpected.

Obviously, I had no means of accessing his bank accounts, but I went into his Excel files in the 'Accounts' directory, where he had kept very disciplined records of income and expenditure. I don't know why he bothered, really, because both were very predictable. And in his later years, he didn't spend on anything much apart from food and books.

The only mild surprise was that he had paid subscriptions to Netflix and Amazon Prime. So, the image of Cedric Waites sitting alone staring at a broken television was perhaps wrong. On the other hand, the subscriptions wouldn't have been any use to him once his broadband had broken down.

That seemed to be it, really. An artist's laptop might be more revelatory. The great novel, the secret symphony . . . Or, at a less dramatic level, the laptop of anyone running a business would have a lot more data on it. But what do ordinary, retired people – even ones who shut themselves up in their houses – use a laptop for?

Email. I went back to the Hotmail account. Maybe there was something I'd missed in the cursory look-through I'd done the previous day. Passionate tell-all letters from a former lover? Threats from a homicidal maniac Cedric had inadvertently offended some decades before?

I didn't just do the Inbox and the Junk. I did Sent Items and Deleted Items as well. Even Archive. Nothing to upset the most hypersensitive of maiden aunts.

One last look back at the Word directories. Travel. Photos. Insurance. Medical. Personal. Accounts. Car (though he didn't seem to have had a car for some time). Christmas Cards (a while since he'd sent any of those, I imagine). Miscellaneous.

I opened random files in the different directories. Their contents provided a kind of outline of a life. Not a very interesting life to the outsider, but no better or worse than most of us go through.

I opened the Accounts directory once again. Documents, filed year by year. 'ACC 1998', 'ACC 2007', 'ACC 2011', 'ACC 2015', 'ACC 2020' and so on. I scrolled down the list.

And then I noticed something odd. The 'ACC' files were Word

documents. Surely, if they actually were accounts, as their names suggested, someone running Microsoft Windows would have used Excel spreadsheet software?

Another anomaly. Some files with the prefix 'XACC'. And they didn't have dates on them, just numbers. The earliest, unsurprisingly, was 'XACC1'.

I clicked 'Open'. A dialogue box told me it was 'Password Protected'.

Trying to keep calm, trying to keep my hands from shaking, I went through the sequence again. 'Flick'. 'Flick1'. 'Flick12'. The file didn't open.

I tried 'Flick123', but I knew I was on a hiding to nothing. I slumped back in despair.

Yes, Ben would probably know a way of breaking in but, having got this far without help, I wanted to crack the code on my own.

I tried to calm myself. I slowed my breathing down, a long-forgotten technique from some yoga class I once went to. I focused on Cedric Waites.

'Flick' had provided the other passwords. Flick had been the dominant force in his adult life. But, suddenly, I remembered that 'Flick' wasn't her given name. Would she have been known as 'Flick' way back when she and Cedric first met?

I deleted my pathetic 'Flick123' from the screen and keyed in 'Felicity'. The file opened. I read.

'Since this is the beginning of a new chapter of my life, I have decided to chronicle it in this exercise book. And to continue chronicling it in further exercise books for as long as I have the good fortune for my marriage to continue.

'Today is the happiest of my life so far. At a ceremony which started at twelve noon in the parish church of St Mary's Pulborough, Felicity Montgomery became Felicity Waites and my wife. After all the unhappiness I went through from my teenage years onwards, the feeling that there was something wrong with me, that I couldn't mix with other people, that I'd never share my life with anyone, that I was destined to be unloved, a reclusive loner whose only companions were his books, all those bad thoughts have gone away. I am married to the woman

I love and, for perhaps the first time in my life, I look forward to the future with undiluted optimism.

'I am writing this in our bedroom at the Old Ship Hotel in Brighton where we are having a honeymoon of three nights (we can't afford more). Felicity thinks I am daft to be writing a diary, but it's something I really want to do and she respects that. I am sure that there will be many funny little quirks we each have and which we will learn to live with as we embark on married life together.

'I am a very fortunate man.'

Given that they were married for over forty years, there were quite a lot of files. The chronicles of their early years pre-dated the availability of computers, which meant that Cedric Waites must have transcribed on to the laptop all the early stuff from the exercise books he mentioned. The task must have taken many, many hours. A labour of love?

Intriguing though this history of a marriage was, I hadn't got time to read every word of it. Need to be selective. There was a strong temptation to go straight to the final entry, to see if he had recorded the provenance of his last meal, the one that killed him.

But I curbed that instinct. I was even more curious to know whether the early bliss of their married life had continued. I thought an interesting junction might be when he changed from writing the diary in longhand in the exercise books to using the laptop. I opened the first of the files with a date on it. Again, the password 'Felicity' did the business.

'I am now writing on this, which is a lot easier – and actually more secure. Though she has to use them at the surgery, Flick has no interest in computers. In the unlikely event of her opening this laptop, I have password-protected this file – and will all the future ones.

'It's also easier to write this diary secretly on the laptop. With the exercise books I always had to hide what I was doing from her – and hide the books too. Whereas on the laptop I could be working on anything. Flick would neither know nor have any interest in what it was. And she wouldn't give me the satisfaction of appearing curious enough to look over my shoulder at what

I'm writing. As she has made clear, she has no interest in anything I do.'

Wow. Love's young dream had certainly soured somewhat. I wondered at what point things had started to go wrong. I returned my attention to the screen and read on.

'Now that I have this laptop, I will transcribe all of my earlier diaries of the marriage. As I finish each exercise book, I will destroy it, probably by burning. Fortunately, Flick's shift patterns mean that there are times when I'm alone in the house and can get on with the transcription. It will be a massive task but the relief of finally knowing for sure that there's no danger of Flick finding the exercise books will more than compensate for the effort.'

When did things change? When did the openness of writing a honeymoon diary in Felicity's presence in Brighton's Old Ship Hotel transform into the paranoia of keeping its entries unseen from Flick?

My experience with hoarders had taught me that a significant change of behaviour frequently follows on from some trauma. I tried to think what major life event might have shaken the Waiteses' marriage to its foundations? All I could think of was the birth of their only child.

This was obviously in one of the numbered files rather than the dated ones. A bit of trial and error, opening files from some fifty years before, enabled me to home in on the entries following Roy's birth (which, incidentally, had taken place at St Richard's in Chichester). Cedric's initial reactions to the new arrival seemed to be that panicky euphoria which afflicts many first-time fathers, a great excitement but also a nervousness about the new responsibility he was taking on, the adjustments that the couple would have to make with a third person in their lives.

It seemed that Felicity Waites had not had an easy labour. She had been kept in hospital for more than a week after the birth to recover, reading between the lines, from a botched episiotomy. I knew – fortunately not from my own experience but from friends and clients – just how painful that could be. Cedric's diary entries showed him to have been concerned and caring

about his wife's condition, but unprepared for the scene that
followed the return of mother and baby to 14 Seacrest Avenue.

'I am still in a state of shock after what Felicity said to me
this afternoon. I know she is in a lot of pain but I do not think
that is what triggered the outburst. She said it was time to talk
about things she had wanted to say for a long time. Almost right
back to the time of our marriage which, she said she now recognized, had been a big mistake.

'I could hardly believe what I was hearing. Felicity said the
mistake she had made was a very old one. Lots of women had
believed that by marrying a man they could change his personality. And, like so many of them, she had been proved wrong.
She said I had always been uncommunicative and self-regarding,
a constant damper on her natural high spirits.

'She also said that she had never enjoyed the sex. And now
that she had done her duty by producing a son – at considerable
cost to her body – there would be no more of "that stuff". She
relied on me to replace our double bed with two singles as soon
as convenient.

'I asked if she meant she wanted a divorce but Felicity said
no. She said she had been brought up to believe in the sanctity
of marriage. Her parents and friends would be appalled if she
got divorced. Besides, it would reflect badly on her judgement.
No, we would stay married. We would go out together as we
had done before. Everyone would continue to think she was the
lively one and I was the quiet one. Outwardly, nothing would
change.

'She said we both had our work to keep us interested in life.
Her only other demands were that I should stop "wasting money
buying books" and that I, "like everyone else who knows me",
should in future always call her "Flick".

'I was absolutely devastated by this sudden change of personality – and perhaps more devastated by the fact that Felicity did
not seem to regard it as a change. It was a revelation of her real
personality. According to her, she was only giving voice to
feelings she had had ever since we got married.

'I'm not an expert on women's health but I know some mothers
can become deeply depressed after giving birth. I wondered
whether this was the cause of my wife's total transformation.

But I've a horrible feeling it isn't. I think she meant everything she said.

'There might have been more but we were interrupted by the crying of our new baby Roy. Felicity said she had to attend to him. Her adaptation to breastfeeding had not gone well, so she went to prepare him a bottle. She gave the impression that it would always be her who took care of our son. She didn't trust me to—'

I was interrupted by hooting from in front of the house. I looked through the window to see a large BMW parked there. Allegra Cramond had emerged from the driver's seat and was waving frantically towards me.

EIGHTEEN

Allegra was, as I might have anticipated, extremely well connected. The family she grew up in was extremely well connected and she extended her network at Oxford University. Straight from there into the Foreign Office. Her various foreign postings seemed to increase rather than diminish the expanding connections she maintained back in the UK. It was no surprise, therefore, when she introduced the expensively suited gentleman in the BMW's passenger seat as Neil Flood, the Deputy Chief Constable of Sussex.

'But please call me Neil,' he said, with suitably well-modulated vowels.

'Neil,' said Allegra, 'is, rather conveniently, a collector of twentieth-century first editions.'

'Just a hobby,' he said modestly.

'I think the way to do it,' said Allegra, 'is for you, Ellen, to go into the shop with Neil.'

'Why?'

'You've been there before. You've met Augustus Mintzen. It would be reasonable for you to introduce a friend who's interested in first editions.'

'My friend being Neil?'

'Of course,' he said with a grin. 'Go back years, don't we?'

'Hm,' I said a little dubiously. I have been guilty of using subterfuge in the past, but I don't like to tell more lies than I have to.

'Is there a problem with that?' asked Allegra. 'Did you part with Augustus Mintzen on bad terms?'

'No, no,' I assured her, glad that I'd resisted using some of the choice lines I'd considered when last in his bookshop. 'No, no, it'll be fine.'

'Good,' said Allegra. 'I'll stay in the car.'

The bell on the door rang as we entered, sounding as corny as ever.

Augustus Mintzen, wearing a brown three-piece tweed suit from the same tailor as the green one, looked up at us over the top of his glasses. 'Good afternoon,' he said.

'Good to see you again,' I said.

'Again?' He gave the impression of having never seen me before in his life.

'I was in the other week to talk about the valuation of Cedric Waites's books.'

'Oh yes, of course. I remember. You're the declutterer, aren't you?'

'That's right. And I was so impressed by your shop,' I lied, 'that I thought I must introduce my friend Neil to it. Neil's a collector of first editions.'

'Oh, excellent,' said Augustus Mintzen, all fuzzy, lovable eccentric.

'Good afternoon,' said Neil with practised charm. 'My particular interest lies in mid-twentieth-century firsts.'

'Well, you've come to the right place. I do have quite a selection of goods that may tempt you. Fiction is it you're after?'

'I have some interest in fiction. Poetry's more my thing.'

'Ah. Well, I have a very nice first of Peter Redgrove's *At the White Monument*. 1963. Signed by the author. Dust jacket in fine condition.' He reached round and his hand instantly found the thin yellowish volume. 'Priced at fifty pounds but we might be able to do a deal.'

'Yes,' said Neil coolly. 'Trouble is I've already got a copy of that.'

'Oh, well done. How clever of you.'

'From another dealer. For twenty-eight pounds.'

'Probably not in such good condition as this one.'

'In perfect condition, actually.'

'Ah. Well. You can always find some dealer having a sale. Anyway, this copy is signed by the poet, so obviously that puts up the price a bit.'

'May I have a look?'

'Of course.' Augustus Mintzen handed the yellow-jacketed slim volume across.

Neil opened it with respectful caution. Over his shoulder I

could read the handwritten inscription. Considerable control was needed for me not to show any emotion.

'And what's the provenance of this?' asked Neil.

'My wife picked it up at a car boot sale,' the bookseller replied evenly. 'This is a very good area for serendipitous discoveries of that kind. The Costa Geriatrica, it gets called. Elderly parents die, their offspring want to empty the house as soon as possible, so that they can sell it. Very few of them are experts in valuation when it comes to books.'

I thought immediately of Roy and Michelle and asked, 'So, has your wife picked up a lot of rare books at car boot sales?'

'She certainly has. She's a very good eye for that kind of bargain. Or maybe I should say "nose"? She sniffs out the valuable ones.'

'Useful wife to have,' said Neil with an easy smile. He held out the catalogue which had been thrust on me at the end of my previous visit to the shop. 'There was something in here that really interested me.'

'Oh yes?'

Neil found the relevant page. '*The Colossus* . . .,' he said.

'Ah.' Augustus Mintzen smiled with satisfaction. 'Sylvia Plath.'

'Exactly.'

'I notice you don't put a price for this in your catalogue. "Available on request".'

'Yes. Because only a serious collector would be contemplating buying the book. We are talking rather a lot of money here.'

'I don't doubt it,' said Neil. 'I am fully aware of the value of a Sylvia Plath first edition.'

'The interest in her and Ted Hughes doesn't seem to diminish. Grows, in fact, all the time. She's become a feminist icon.'

'And he the paradigm of unfaithful husbands,' said Neil.

'That's the way it is, yes,' Augustus Mintzen agreed. 'They're a bit like the Bloomsbury Group. As with Virginia Woolf's, people would pay thousands for one of Sylvia Plath's shopping lists.'

'And for a first edition of her first book of poems, with handwritten dedication . . .?'

'They would pay many, many thousands.'

'Hm.' Neil nodded thoughtfully. 'Well, I am a serious collector, fully aware of the current market value of a Sylvia Plath first edition. And I am seriously interested in purchasing the copy you have for sale.'

'Excellent.' Augustus Mintzen didn't actually rub his hands together, but he had the look of a man who wanted to.

'So, Mr Mintzen, might it be possible for me to see the goods on offer?'

'Of course. Because of the rarity of this particular volume, I keep it in my safe.'

'Very sensible.'

'You will excuse me a moment while I get it.'

'Of course.'

Left alone, I looked across at Neil. He put a discreet finger to his lips, indicating that we could talk about anything other than the Sylvia Plath first edition.

'Regular treasure trove in here, isn't it?' I said, looking around the shelves.

'Yes. Thank you so much for introducing me to it. Sadly, bookshops like this are becoming increasingly rare. So much of the trade is done online these days.'

Pretty uncontroversial conversation. If Augustus Mintzen had overheard it, no harm would have been done.

He bustled self-importantly back in, bearing a neat cardboard box. Before opening it, he reached into a drawer and produced a rather grubby pair of white gloves which, with appropriate ceremony, he proceeded to put on.

The precious volume was swathed in white tissue paper. The ceremony with which he unwrapped it would have been appropriate for an Egyptian mummy. He laid the book on the tissue paper on his desk.

Neil looked at it with awe. If his reaction was manufactured, then he was a very good actor. But I got the impression that he was genuinely moved to be looking at such a rarity.

'And dare I ask, Mr Mintzen,' he said, 'how much you are asking for the book?'

The bookseller glowed with self-esteem as he replied, 'Comparing it with recent sales of similar Sylvia Plath works,' he pronounced judiciously, 'I could not let it go for less than thirty-five thousand pounds.'

Neil was not shocked by the answer. He nodded thoughtfully,

as a genuine collector of Sylvia Plath – and perhaps he was one
– would have done.

'You said there was an inscription . . .?'

'Yes.'

'You open it, Mr Mintzen. You've got the gloves on.'

The bookseller did as instructed. Like Neil, I peered down at
the handwritten inscription on the title page. Once again, I had
to curb my natural reaction of excitement.

'Wonderful, actually to see Sylvia Plath's writing,' said Neil.
'I still get a frisson seeing something that I know has been touched
by one of my favourite writers.'

'Oh, I agree.' Augustus Mintzen beamed. 'It's for just such
moments that I went into the book-dealing business.'

'Yes.' Neil nodded. There was a silence, then he said, 'Strange,
that both the Sylvia Plath and the Peter Redgrove have the same
dedicatee.'

'Perhaps not that strange,' said the bookseller. 'Must have
come from some private collection that the children of the owner
wanted to get rid of in a hurry.'

'Possibly,' said Neil. 'Did your wife find them at the same car
boot sale?'

'I can't remember,' said Augustus Mintzen. 'Maybe she did.
I just remember being extraordinarily excited when she came
back with the Sylvia Plath.'

'I'm sure you were,' said Neil drily. 'But you don't know if
your wife got them at the same car boot sale?'

'No.'

'Well, maybe you could ask her . . .?'

'Yes. Perhaps I could.'

'Or I could tell you myself.' A new voice, belonging to the
woman who suddenly materialized from the stockroom. It was
the second time I had seen her in the shop. Rosemary Findlay.

We all introduced ourselves. Rosemary clearly knew who I
was but she made no comment.

'We've just been hearing,' said Neil Flood charmingly, 'about
your incredible luck at picking up valuable books at car boot
sales.'

'It's not luck,' she said rather sniffily. 'Thanks to Gus's work,
I do know rather a lot about books. Very few people who attend

car boot sales do. Which means I'm well placed to pick up the bargains when I see them.'

'So . . .' Neil smiled. 'Your husband seems unable to remember. Maybe you can help us. Did you pick up the Peter Redgrove and the Sylvia Plath at the same car boot sale?'

'I'm afraid I can't remember either.'

'It just seems a strange coincidence,' Neil Flood went on, 'that both books are dedicated to the same person. Someone called "Mim".'

'Then that would suggest,' said Rosemary, as if the idea had only just occurred to her, 'that they did come from the same collection.'

Neil nodded. 'Yes, I'd have thought so.' A reassuring grin. 'And you've no idea who this "Mim" might be?'

Rosemary shook her head.

Her husband chipped in, 'I have done extensive research into the matter. Consulted biographies of both Sylvia Plath and Ted Hughes. Couldn't find any reference to someone in their circle called "Mim".'

'Just coincidence then?' Neil suggested.

'It must be,' said Rosemary coolly.

'No other explanation,' Gus agreed.

'No.' Then suddenly Neil Flood's tone changed. The charming book collector turned into the Deputy Chief Constable of Sussex. 'Except there is an explanation, a very simple one. These books weren't found at any car boot sale. They were stolen from the home of their rightful owner, Mim Galbraith.'

'Nonsense!' said Rosemary Findlay.

'That can't be right,' said Augustus Mintzen. And the way he looked at his wife suggested that he had, until that moment, believed her story about the serendipitous discoveries at car boot sales.

'Mim Galbraith,' the policeman went on, 'was part of Ted Hughes's and Sylvia Plath's circle in the 1950s. Peter Redgrove was another poet in the group. These two books were dedicated to her.'

'Have you any proof of that?' asked a brazen Rosemary Findlay.

'Mim Galbraith will vouch for it.'

'Mim Galbraith has got dementia. Her testimony is worthless. It would never stand up in court.'

'No?' said Neil. 'She clearly remembers you coming to her house.'

I couldn't stop myself from saying, 'Pretending to be a legitimate declutterer.'

Still, Rosemary Findlay was unfazed. 'I know what you're doing, Mr Flood. Book collectors are always like this. You'll try anything to beat a dealer down on price. So, you create this fanciful story about the provenance of the books, claiming they're stolen, in the hope of knocking a few thousand off the asking price. Well, I'm afraid that little ploy won't work with us. Gus and I will have no problem in finding a less devious buyer for the books.

'And now I must ask you to leave. And take your pathetic stories with you. If you really believe the nonsense you're telling us . . .' She was almost jeering now, her words larded with sarcasm '. . . why don't you get in touch with the police? They'll be really interested in the testimony of a demented old woman, won't they?'

'Do you know, Mrs Mintzen,' said Neil Flood, 'I think they really will be.'

And he told her his true identity, as Deputy Chief Constable of Sussex.

That did take the wind out of her sails.

Lunchtime had come and gone. I wasn't interested in food. All I wanted to do was get back to Chichester and Cedric Waites's diary. I was silently urging Allegra to exceed the speed limit, but she was far too responsible to do that.

My mobile rang. Normally I wouldn't have taken a call in someone else's car. But the display told me it was from Ben. I always take calls from Ben. Particularly after what had happened on the Saturday night. I answered.

'Ma,' he said, his voice urgent and excited, 'Jools and I have found Dodge. But he won't come with us. Can you try and persuade him?'

NINETEEN

Ben and Jools were waiting in the Morris Commer CV9/40 Tipper van at West Stoke car park. It somehow felt wrong to see anyone other than Dodge in its driver's seat.

They quickly brought me up to speed with their progress. Through Pat, in Portsmouth that morning they had contacted another young man, Jared, who'd also been helped by Dodge with his drug problems. Part of the treatment had involved getting out of the urban environment to walk in the countryside. Dodge had taken the young man to the nature reserve of Kingley Vale, a forest of yew trees, said to be some of the oldest living things in Britain. I knew it well. Only a few miles north-west of Chichester, it was a favourite destination for Ben and Juliet in their pre-teen years. They would spend hours climbing on the tangle of ancient branches. There was something magical about the place, though it was not an entirely benign magic.

Jared had told them how Dodge had talked about living in the wild and foraging. He had shown him a copse within Kingley Vale which would be suitable for such an experiment. Jared had a very exact recollection of where it was and gave Ben and Jools directions.

They had followed these and found minimal evidence of Dodge's presence in a small clearing at the centre of the copse. His woodcraft skills were highly developed and nobody who hadn't been looking for traces of human occupation would have observed anything untoward.

Wandering through the woods nearby, they had seen Dodge. Kingley Vale was much visited by walkers, families and tourists. So, the fugitive had to keep on the move during the day, mingling with the visitors, looking as though he had some purpose other than self-concealment. At nights he homed in on his burrow.

It was a hazardous way of life and I didn't think Dodge could survive there long. Oh, he might be able to forage enough to eat, but there were a lot of wardens around such a popular tourist site. It was only a matter of time before the frequency of sightings of the stranger would make someone suspicious. An arrest for trespass wasn't going to help Dodge's avoidance of contact with the police.

Ben and Jools didn't have any difficulty in finding him again, which reinforced my view that he was soon going to alert the nature reserve's authorities. Dodge looked pretty dreadful. Not as if he was starving or ill, but very dirty and paranoid. He always avoided eye contact, now he appeared deeply distressed.

'Come back with us, Dodge,' I wheedled. 'You'll be safe at my place.'

He shook his head. 'The police are on to you. They'll be watching your place.'

'They really won't,' I said. 'They no longer have any interest in me.'

I was on a hiding to nothing. He was determined to stay in Kingley Vale. Until he was evicted from the place or arrested. I kept telling him those were the only two possible outcomes, but he wouldn't listen.

'You can't stay here for ever, Dodge,' I said eventually. 'You're going to get caught by the rangers.'

'No. I can keep out of their way.'

'And what will make you come back, Dodge?' I asked, almost despairing.

'I'll come back when the police know who poisoned Cedric Waites. And know for certain that I didn't,' he pronounced definitively.

Getting back to Cedric's diary became even more urgent. I hope to God it would provide the information that I needed.

Ben and Jools said they were going to stop at a pub on the way back. I bit back my instinct to say I hoped whoever was driving didn't drink. It would be Ben inevitably, and he would.

So, I arrived back home on my own. And went straight to the laptop.

No faffing around this time. I went straight to the final entry.

'Spent most of the day going through book catalogues online. There's a first of Eric Ambler's *The Mask of Dimitrios* which quite interests me. No dust jacket and they're asking £850. Seems a bit steep. On the other hand, what else have I got to spend money on? It doesn't matter much how much is left when I go. Heated up one of the home-cooked meals from the freezer for supper. A bit too veggie for my taste.'

I groaned inwardly. Why on earth hadn't Cedric Waites described his 'last supper' in more detail?

My investigation seemed to have hit the buffers. I felt frustrated, tantalized. To have actually found the reference I was searching for, but for it to have denied me the information I needed . . . I tried to replace my disappointment with logic.

Another approach was required. The cause of Cedric Waites's death was the major fact I was searching for, but the diaries could still yield other information about his life. The fact that he had kept them a secret from his wife suggested potentially combustible contents.

I wondered what he had written about Flick's death. I knew the year that had happened, so it would be in one of the dated files. I scrolled through the entries. Six weeks, I remembered being told, from the diagnosis of pancreatic cancer to the end.

In June, Cedric's entries suddenly became much shorter. Just notes, really. Records of hospital visits. 'Flick seems a lot weaker.' 'The consultant tells me it's only a matter of time.' Just facts, no emotional reactions, no indications of Cedric's feelings about what was happening.

Then I got to the day of his wife's death.

'I have just come back from St Richard's, having left Felicity there for the last time. I'm sure my reactions will, in time, become more complex, but all I feel now is relief. Huge relief. And not, I'm afraid, worthy relief that my wife's sufferings are at an end. No, my relief comes from the knowledge that I will never have to spend another minute with her.

'I must ring Roy soon and tell him. Or, rather, tell Michelle. She always answers the phone. I sometimes wonder if there's some kind of hereditary curse that has forced my son into exactly the same kind of marriage that I had. Maybe I'm wrong about that, though. They always say you can never know what goes on inside another marriage. Perhaps the sex is terrific. Though, having looked at Michelle, I doubt it.

'Anyway, now I can get on with the life I should have had, not the life I've wasted for God knows how many decades. And that life will involve the absolute minimum of bloody people!

'The thought that I will never have to go to another social event and watch silently while Felicity charms the pants off everyone in the room . . . well, I could weep for joy.

'Don't know whether I need to change my will now that she's gone. I'll check with the solicitors. They're a dozy bunch but should know enough to be able to tell me that. I've lined up Tim Goodrich to be my executor and, in spite of his shortcomings in other areas of his life, I'm sure he'll do that efficiently enough.

'Roy and Michelle will have to come down for the funeral, but once they've gone, I intend not to allow anyone else inside the house. I'm sure that cow Michelle imagines that they'll be sole beneficiaries when I do finally pop my clogs. Pity I won't be able to witness the expression on her face when she finds out they get nothing. Feel a bit rotten doing the dirty on Roy, but it's his own fault. He shouldn't have married the bitch. That's where his life went wrong, just as mine did when I married Felicity.'

There was a lot of information there, but I'm afraid the phrase that stuck with me was, in relation to Tim Goodrich, 'in spite of his shortcomings in other areas of his life'. Right then, that was more important to me than a detail like who killed Cedric Waites.

I remembered Tim telling me that he and Flick had had a joint retirement party. With foreboding, I scrolled back some six weeks from the entry following her death and found the right day.

'Just back from Felicity's retirement party. Conservatory area at the back of the George and Dragon in North Street. God, it was ghastly. Felicity all over everyone, hugging and kissing. Everyone telling me how marvellous she was, Flick this, Flick that, what a loss she would be to the practice. It made me feel sick.

'Had a sensible conversation with Tim Goodrich. The party was also to mark his leaving the practice. Bit of a smoothie, but I like him. Going to do a PhD in Oxford, apparently. Rumours, though, that he was leaving the practice under something of a cloud. Talk of him being over-familiar with some of his female patients. I don't know about that, but he certainly has a reputation for coming on to anything in a skirt. According to Felicity, his infidelities broke up his marriage. Wife had had enough and upped sticks.

'Seeing him with Felicity, all very huggy and snuggly, made me wonder for a moment whether there had ever been anything going on there, between the two of them. But I don't think so. Though she's always like that in a crowd, I think alone with any man, she'd be as frigid as she is with me. Felicity doesn't do sex.'

I felt numb with shock. Stupid. And naïve. To think I was so unpractised in the world of relationships to believe the sincerity of a well-known lothario. I choked back the urge to vomit.

I scrolled desultorily through a few more files, feeling only shame.

TWENTY

Detective Inspector Bayles sat behind his desk, looking cosy and avuncular, but also dubious. 'I agree, it could mean that. But it's not what you'd call hard evidence. If we actually had the container which the meal was in . . .'

Yes, all right. Rub it in. I was never going to be allowed to forget my destruction of the evidence.

'Anyway,' he went on, 'I don't know how much longer we can put resources into this investigation.'

'You mean you're closing the case?' I was appalled. In most of the crime series I saw on television, the police were relentlessly tenacious. A setback in a case served only as an invitation to redouble their efforts to nail the criminal.

'Everything takes time,' he explained. 'Time means man-hours in a force that's already stretched almost to breaking point. So, we have to prioritize. And the death of one elderly man . . . which might have been murder . . . well, the investigation could take a long time and come up with nothing.'

'"Might have been murder",' I echoed. 'You seemed convinced it was murder when we last spoke.'

'Ellen, Ellen,' he said wearily. 'We in the police are not in the habit of abandoning investigations at the drop of a hat. Things stay on file. Cold cases do get revived – if they didn't, half of the output of television crime series wouldn't exist. But, as I say, it's a matter of resources. Also, the likelihood of getting a conviction. And I tell you, the Crown Prosecution Service would not recommend pressing charges on the basis of what you've shown me from that laptop. A baby barrister still in pupillage could tear the prosecution case apart in no time.

'I'm sorry, Ellen. What you're telling me may well be right. You may have fingered the murderer of Cedric Waites. But the chances of getting a conviction are so infinitesimal as to be invisible. So, I will effectively be closing the investigation . . . unless you can provide me with more solid evidence for the accusation you're making.'

It was displacement activity, really. Sooner or later, I had to contact Tim Goodrich. The man I had so nearly gone to bed with. The man who had inherited half of Cedric Waites's estate.

But there was something else that needed doing. It was late afternoon. Still time to perform a necessary good deed.

The walk from West Stoke car park seemed to take longer this time. I felt a bit light-headed. I hadn't had anything to eat since breakfast. And the information I had received about Tim Goodrich had unsettled me a great deal.

There was a ranger at the entrance to Kingley Vale. 'Sorry, madam,' he said. 'Not letting anyone else in today. Come back tomorrow, by all means.'

'I've come to fetch someone who's hiding in the woods.'

The man chuckled. 'No one can hide in here. We check over every square inch of the place. Oh, people try it on. Travellers, would-be campers, people setting up illegal barbecues. We flush them all out.'

'There is someone in here. I can lead you to them.'

The ranger looked dubious. Then, he conceded, 'All right. But I bet we don't find anyone.'

He called out to a colleague to watch the entrance, and we set off.

It said a lot for Dodge's woodcraft skills that he had evaded the rangers' vigilance for so long. Even when we were right beside the copse he had hidden in, there was no sign of habitation. He'd made a burrow covered with yew branches. If I hadn't known him to be there, I would have moved on to look elsewhere.

I called gently to him. 'Dodge, it's Ellen. It's all right. The police are not pursuing the case any more.'

That shook the ranger. 'Is he wanted by the police?'

'No, it's a misunderstanding. Dodge, come out,' I said, very softly.

And he did. There was a considerable rustling of grass and twigs, then the tall, dishevelled figure appeared.

'How long have you been there?' asked the aggrieved ranger.
Dodge started. He'd expected me to be on my own.

'Don't worry,' I soothed. 'You can go home now. The police
are no longer looking for anyone.'

As we walked back to the entrance, the ranger talked grumpily
about trespass, but he didn't suggest any further action being
taken. I think he was divided between annoyance and admiration
for Dodge's concealment skills.

Back in the Yeti, I told Dodge I was worried he might have
done a runner again when he saw me.

'No,' he said. 'You told me the police had closed the case.'

'Yes, but—'

'And I knew you wouldn't lie.'

Dodge didn't say anything after that, just a mumbled 'Thank
you', when I deposited him at his place.

'Your van, incidentally,' I said, 'is no longer in Portsmouth.'

A moment of alarm. 'Have the police got it?'

'No. Ben's got it.'

'Ah.'

'We'll get it back to you as soon as we can.'

'Thank you.'

'Well, see you soon.'

'Ellen . . .'

'Yes?'

'I'd never have put oleander by mistake into anything I cooked
for Cedric.'

'I know, Dodge. And I can assure you that, whoever did put
it in the meal, they did so very definitely on purpose.'

What I now knew about Tim Goodrich made calling him easier
rather than more difficult. I had no emotional anxiety about his
response. I just felt huge relief not to have got closer to him than
I had.

He answered the phone immediately. He must have put my
number into his address book because he knew immediately it
was me.

'Very nice to hear you, Ellen,' he oozed. 'Sorry our last
encounter got rather . . . nipped in the bud. I hope things were

all right at home. And I hope you're ringing to ask whether we can pick up where we left off.'

'No,' I said flatly. 'That's not why I'm ringing. Are you still in Chichester?'

'I am, actually. Staying at least till tomorrow afternoon. Roy and Michelle are coming down. They insist on having a meeting with me and Vi Spelling.'

'Do you know why?'

'I think there's a good chance they want to contest Cedric's will. Claim he wasn't in his right mind when he drew it up, something like that. Maybe appeal to our better natures, see if Vi and I are prepared to agree some compromise with them.'

'And is that likely to happen?'

'Good God, no. I don't have a better nature.'

It was said as a joke, and I might have found it funny before I read the diary. I didn't pass any comment, just asked, 'Where will you be meeting them?'

'At the house. Seacrest Avenue. Handy for Vi. Eleven o'clock.'

'I'll be there,' I said. 'I've still got a key.'

'Oh. Very well. I can't stop you. So . . . I'm going to be in Chichester this evening. You're going to be in Chichester this evening. Maybe we could pick up where—'

'No,' I said.

In fact, that evening Ben drove the Commer van back to Dodge's and I followed in the Yeti to bring him back.

Dodge was grateful but still subdued. He didn't invite us in for nettle tea.

I was worried about the effect his recent trauma had had on him.

Mind you, I could say the same about Ben.

And Jools, come to that.

But I was more worried about what was going to happen the next morning.

It was a long time since there had been so many people in the front room of 14 Seacrest Avenue. Jools and I had moved the furniture out into the hall ready for disposal at various charities, but by the time I arrived two armchairs had been moved back in. Vi

Spelling and Michelle Waites were sitting in them. I was reminded that there are very few people whom pink hair suits. Roy and Tim were perched on piled-up boxes of books. The atmosphere was not relaxed.

Michelle looked up at my arrival. 'What the hell are you doing here?'

'I have an interest in what went on,' I replied, sounding cooler than I felt. 'And you may recall, you did employ me to clear the house.'

'Yes, but when I employed you, I thought the house would belong to Roy and me. If you think I'm going to pay for your services in a house that doesn't belong to me, then think again.'

'Don't worry, Ellen,' said Tim. 'I'll see you get paid.'

'Fine,' said Michelle, still seething. 'I never realized the old fool would make such a stupid will. He must have been demented. Surely you can challenge a will if it's made by someone not in their right mind?'

'You can,' said Tim, 'but, according to the solicitors, Cedric was very definitely in his right mind when he made the will.'

'I'm sure he really meant everything to go to Roy and me,' Michelle pleaded.

'The terms of his will,' Tim pointed out, 'would suggest the exact opposite. Rather than going to you, he preferred that his estate should be divided between two people he didn't know very well but who had shown him kindness. Something which,' he added with considerable edge, 'according to Cedric, you and Roy never did.'

'That's not fair,' Michelle protested. 'We offered him kindness and he rejected it. After Flick's funeral, I sent meals for him to freeze and . . .' She stopped herself.

'Did you?' asked Tim. 'So, we have three people in this room, all of whom cooked meals for Cedric. Interesting. All suspects, you might say. I'm the only one,' he added smugly, 'who isn't a suspect. I never cooked anything for Cedric Waites.'

'Well, I cooked for him,' said Vi Spelling, 'and I know there was never anything poisonous in anything I cooked. Because I always ate the same things, just did an extra portion for Cedric. And I'm still here. If one of my meals done for him, then it must have been because he didn't freeze it properly and he got that bottleism.'

'Botulism,' Tim corrected her. 'Except that Cedric wasn't killed by botulism. He was poisoned by oleander.'

'Well, it wasn't in anything I give him,' said Vi definitively. She turned a fierce gaze on Michelle. 'And if you think I'm going to give up what Cedric left me in his will, think again. I'm not saying I wasn't surprised, but if that's what he wanted to do, then that's up to him. I respect his wishes.'

Feeling the eyes of Roy and Michelle on him, Tim said, 'I feel exactly the same as Vi. I'm not going to raise the issue of deserving. I'm sure I don't deserve what Cedric left me. But it was his decision and I, like Vi, will respect his wishes.'

Time for a change of subject. I announced, 'I saw Detective Inspector Bayles yesterday. He told me the police are giving up the investigation into Cedric's death.'

The relief this brought to Roy and Michelle was palpable. 'It was always pointless,' he said. 'No one deliberately poisoned Dad.'

'Of course they didn't,' Michelle agreed.

'The inspector told me,' I said, 'that the case would go on file and only be revived if there was evidence of the crime strong enough to stand up in court.'

'Which there never will be,' said Michelle. 'Pity the container from which he took his final meal was never found.'

Was that a deliberate shot at me? I couldn't be sure. How could she have known that I had taken the containers to the dump?

Time to throw petrol on the dying fire. 'Did you know,' I asked, 'that Cedric kept a diary?'

'No,' said Michelle.

'I'm sure he didn't,' said Roy.

'Oh, he did. On his laptop.'

'He didn't have a laptop.'

'Oh, he did,' I said again. 'My daughter found it when she was helping with the clearance here. And,' I went on, 'in his diary he had interesting things to say about all three of you.'

'Me too?' asked Tim, surprised and a little taken aback.

'Yes, he had a lot to say about you.' I let a silence elapse before I said, 'And, in the diary's final entry, Cedric said what he ate for his last meal.'

'I'm sure he didn't!' Roy burst out.

'Oh, he did. Every day he detailed what he'd had for supper. And his . . . "last supper", shall we call it . . . was a vegetarian meal.'

'Then I didn't cook it,' said Vi. 'Vegetables are meant to go *with* things, not be meals in their own right.'

'Michelle,' I said, 'you said you cooked some meals for Cedric after Flick's funeral . . .?'

'We're talking eight years ago. And I never got any thanks from him, so I stopped sending them.'

'Were any of those meals vegetarian?'

'Possibly. I can't remember.'

'And do you grow oleander in your garden in Worcester?'

'No,' said Michelle defiantly.

'Oh, now come on, love,' came a gentle interpolation from her husband. 'There's no point in lying. You'll just make people suspicious of you where there's no cause. You have mentioned having oleander in the garden.'

'What do you know about it? You do bugger all in the garden!'

'Oh, that's not fair. I do the mowing and the digging.'

'But I do the artistic side of it. That's all down to me.'

'Yes, love. I'm not going to argue about that.' He spoke as if he'd closed the subject, but then continued, 'And it's just silly to lie about us having oleander in the garden.' He chuckled. 'You remember, at one stage you talked about sending an oleander salad to your Enemy Number One, Bobbi.'

'I didn't.'

Roy, who seemed to find what he was telling amusing, explained for his audience, 'Bobbi's a particularly unpleasant academic who works at the same university we do – or I do and Michelle did. She organized things so that Michelle got sacked, though it's gone to a tribunal and I'm confident that she'll get her job back.'

'You don't know that,' snapped Michelle.

'As I say, I'm quietly confident, love. Anyway, I don't need to tell you that Bobbi is not Flavour of the Month chez Waites. And Michelle, quite understandably, swore all kinds of revenges on her. One of which . . .' he chuckled again, 'was sending her an oleander salad!

'Well, I knew how furious Michelle was, but I did tell her that that wasn't the right way of going about things. Wait for the findings of the tribunal, I said, then everything'll be sorted out.'

'Like hell it will,' said Michelle bitterly.

'And,' I asked, 'did Michelle get as far as making the . . . "oleander salad"?'

'She went through the motions,' Roy replied.

'What do you mean by that?'

'She got everything prepared on the kitchen work surface – the oleander, the other ingredients, a container to put the meal in.'

'Didn't you try to stop her?' asked Tim.

Roy shook his head sagaciously. 'Oh no, I know my wife too well for that. Even Michelle herself would admit she's got a temper on her. Haven't you, love?' His wife did not respond. 'Anyway, experience – painful experience at times – has taught me not to tackle Michelle at the height of her fury, but wait till she calms down. Then you can have a rational conversation with her. So, I waited till she'd finished the salad and packed it neatly in its plastic container – and then I told her why there was no way she could give it to Bobbi.'

'Why not?' I asked.

'Because . . .' Roy beamed at his own cleverness '. . . unbeknownst to Michelle, I had filmed her making the salad on my phone!'

On a note of triumph, he continued, 'And when Michelle realized I had evidence, she began to see the funny side. Yes, Bobbi was a cow who would get her comeuppance in time, but there was no need for Michelle to take risks in trying to get a private revenge. I think I manged the situation rather well,' he concluded complacently.

'So, what happened to the container with the salad in it?' I asked.

Roy shrugged. 'Don't know. I assume Michelle binned it.'

'And how long ago was this?' asked Tim.

'Few weeks back, month maybe.' Roy turned to his wife. 'I remember, it was a day before you went down to London for those lectures on gender dysphoria.'

'That's right,' said Michelle dismissively. She rose from her chair. 'The only reason we're here this morning is to see whether you two . . .' she cast accusatory looks at Tim and Vi '. . . would admit the invalidity of Cedric's will. Since you clearly won't, we may have to consult solicitors about the situation.'

'It won't do you any good,' said Tim. 'And you know it.'

'We'll see.' Michelle Waites spoke with more bravado than logic. 'Right, Roy, I think we should be on our way.'

'Just a minute,' I said. A memory was crystallizing in my mind. Of the time when I had first met Vi Spelling, when she had tapped on the Yeti's window outside this very house. And how she'd ended our conversation that day. I reminded her of the occasion.

'Yes, yes, I remember it,' she said. 'I'm not senile, you know.'

'And back then, Vi,' I went on, 'you mentioned that you'd seen Michelle down here another time, since Flick's funeral.'

'I told you,' said Michelle icily, 'we stayed down here for a while afterwards.'

'I'm talking about more recently.'

The pleading look I'd turned on Vi produced immediate results. 'Oh yes, I remember. I seen her only a few weeks back.'

'I'm sure you didn't,' said Michelle, defying argument.

'Comes back to me,' Vi insisted. 'Must've been a Tuesday or a Thursday . . . because I delivered a meal to Cedric's back doorstep. And when I got there . . .' she slowed down as she took in the implication of her words '. . . there was another food container already there . . . and what's more, my fiver had gone.'

She faced Michelle. 'You. You put it there.'

Cedric's daughter-in-law looked around and saw no sympathy in any of the faces. 'What if I did? I was only doing what Roy had told me to do.'

Her husband stared at her in shock. But his wife turned on him. 'I told you it was a bad idea! He would have died soon enough, anyway. We only had to wait.'

'Except, of course,' Tim pointed out, 'what you were waiting for never existed. Cedric had already decided you weren't going to benefit at all from his estate.'

'That's not the point,' said Michelle.

'I would have thought it was very much the point,' argued

Tim. 'If Roy asked you to deliver a poisoned meal to his father, we're talking about murder.'

'Maybe,' Michelle grinned grimly. 'But Ellen said the police have shelved the case.'

'Until they get more solid evidence.'

'Sorry to disappoint you, Tim, but they haven't got more solid evidence.'

'No, Michelle? You've just said that Roy told you to deliver the poisoned meal to his father.'

'Coerced me more like. Anyway, whatever he did, it doesn't change the situation.'

'No?'

'No. Because I would never testify against Roy. Which means that, so far as Detective Inspector Bayles's investigation goes, things haven't advanced at all. There's no proof, only conjecture.'

There was a long silence. Then Roy Waites spoke. And he spoke with a vehemence I had never expected from him, a vehemence that implied painful years of saying nothing. 'I can't let this go on! Blaming me for planning the murder won't wash. It was you, Michelle, all you!'

His wife was so taken aback by this sudden transformation of his character that she was momentarily lost for words. It didn't matter. Roy had plenty.

'You talked about doing it, but I never thought you would. Since Bobbi kicked you out of your job, you've been obsessed about money. You talked about "hurrying Dad on his way", but I didn't think you were serious. And all in the hope of winning a jackpot that didn't exist.

'Dad was ahead of the game, though. It wasn't me he wanted to cut out of his will, it was you. He knew if I inherited anything, you would only take it from me. Just as you have taken so much else from my life.

'It's ironic, really, to see how I made exactly the same mistake as Dad. We both married women who were as cold as ice, women who were bright and cheerful with other people, reserving all their hatred for their husbands.

'My parents went as far as having a child. How often I wish they hadn't. But no, you ruled out that scenario, didn't you, Michelle? At first, I was disappointed, but soon I became grateful that we didn't have a child, someone who might suffer as I did when I was growing up. You can't imagine the stress of living in a household where, if ever there was an outsider present, the parents would maintain a front of togetherness. And the instant they were alone, or alone with me, the shoutings and recriminations started. Not from Dad. He didn't say much. No, all the bile came out of the mouth of the universally loved Flick.' He put a lifetime of bitterness into the name.

'Can you imagine what it was like to grow up in a household when you never saw your parents touch each other unless there was someone else present?

'And to think I was fool enough to make exactly the same mistake. Maybe it's just something that happens if you grow up seeing no evidence that a woman could ever be nice to a man? Was it some death wish that made me seek out a woman identical to my mother?'

'I'm nothing like your mother!' Michelle protested.

'You are where it matters,' Roy bellowed. 'You are in your inability to love anyone but yourself!'

'Well, I hope you've enjoyed venting your spleen,' said Michelle, in the manner of someone calling a recalcitrant puppy to order. 'We'll talk about this further when we get home. When there are less people listening,' she added pointedly.

'I don't think you'll be going home for a while, Michelle,' said Roy. 'I think you may be having a rather uncomfortable interview with Detective Inspector Bayles.'

'Nonsense! As Ellen has pointed out, whatever conjectures you care to spread about, there is still no solid evidence against anyone.'

'Really?' said her husband, suddenly icy cool. 'I'm thinking you're forgetting I still have on my phone the footage of you preparing the meal with the oleander in it.'

'I don't believe you!'

'It's true. And I made a note of it in my diary.'

'Diary? You don't keep a diary!'

'Oh, I do.'

'Since when?'

'Since I realized what a terrible mistake I'd made in marrying you. So let's say . . . since our honeymoon.'

I was beginning to wonder how many more parallels there would be between father and son in this chronicle of misery.

'The fact that you made a diary entry,' Michelle spat out, 'is still not solid proof.'

'The phone footage might be more convincing, though,' he said, 'particularly when taken with Vi's testimony that she saw you down here on the day an unexplained food container appeared on the back doorstep.'

'But Roy . . .' She was weeping now, hot tears of frustration. 'You wouldn't shop me to the police, would you?'

She moved towards him. He recoiled, as if from some venomous snake. 'Yes, I would, Michelle. My mother tried to raise a barrier between me and my dad. You did exactly the same. But neither of you could change what I felt for him. And I'd certainly shop to the police anyone who killed the only person I ever loved.'

Michelle Waites was docile while I rang Detective Inspector Bayles. He sounded sceptical but sufficiently interested to want to see her. He offered to send a car but Roy said he'd drive her to the police station. I hoped to God that, on the short journey, she wouldn't manage to reassert her iron control over him.

But I wasn't really worried. Roy Waites had changed for life. I wonder if he too would become a recluse, living alone and not letting any outsider into the house in Worcester.

Their departure, of course, left me and Tim Goodrich alone in the sitting room,

'What you read in Cedric's diary,' he said, 'presumably referred to my reputation in Chichester as something of a ladies' man . . .?'

'Yes.'

'I'm not trying to exonerate myself,' he said. 'I did behave pretty badly back then.'

'Right.'

'I have changed.'

I grinned ruefully. 'Two things I've learnt. One, the obvious – women always think they can change men. And they can't. Second – never believe a man who says he's changed. Because he hasn't.'

'Fair enough. Harsh, but I suppose fair enough.' He turned on me a look which, the previous week, would have melted my resistance. 'My attraction to you is genuine. I'm not making it up.'

'My attraction to you was genuine too.'

'"Was"?'

'Yes. Was.'

'Hm.' He seemed to take that on board. 'I must get back to Oxford.'

'Where there must be at least one avid graduate student waiting for you.'

'That'd be telling,' he said, with some of his old bravado. 'Well, I'll be on my way.' He moved towards the door, then stopped. 'I was thinking, Ellen, what broke up what was promising to be a pleasant evening on Saturday . . .'

'Yes?'

'. . . was an SOS from your son.'

'Via my daughter, yes.'

'Family's always going to come first with you, Ellen.'

'I'm afraid you're right, Tim.'

'And family still includes your late husband.'

I couldn't deny it. He was right there too. Damn it.

TWENTY-ONE

'This is a poem I love,' said Mim Galbraith, flicking through her beloved first edition of *The Colossus and Other Poems*. '"Watercolour of Grantchester Meadows". I remember Sylvia actually reading it in Grantchester. Ted was there . . . Peter Redgrove . . . and . . . Oh God, what was the name of the man I was sleeping with then? I can't remember.' She was unfazed by the lapse. 'No, great loss, anyway.'

Allegra Cramond chuckled. The sun streamed into the sitting room, where we were having coffee. The stolen books had been restored. Mim would not have been interested to know that the volume in her hand was worth over thirty thousand pounds. She cherished it as a book, nothing else. Books, after all, as she said again, had been the continuity of her life.

Rosemary Findlay and Augustus Mintzen had both been arrested. Police investigations had revealed that Mim was not the only victim of their thefts. Rosemary had filched a good few other treasures from houses where she had been decluttering. She had chosen her targets carefully. Only people with dementia, unlikely to notice the loss of the odd book, or unlikely to be believed if they did draw attention to it.

According to Allegra, at first Augustus Mintzen had claimed to have nothing to do with the crime. He thought his wife just had a lot of luck at car boot sales. But, as the police enquiries proceeded, urged on by Neil Flood who was a genuine book-lover, it became clear that the two of them had been working together on the scheme. The shop in Petworth was unceremoniously closed, and Augustus Mintzen lost any credibility that he might have had in the world of antiquarian books. Both he and his wife received substantial prison sentences.

I was particularly annoyed by what they'd done. Rogue operators like Rosemary Findlay do nothing for the image of the noble decluttering profession.

That morning, as we drank coffee at Mim's, Dodge was there,

putting the final touches to her revitalized bookshelves. The evenness of the rows of books covering the walls made me proud of the job that Jools and I had done there.

'This is a poem I love,' said Mim Galbraith, lifting up the book again. '"Watercolour of Grantchester Meadows". I remember Sylvia actually reading it in Grantchester. Ted was there . . .'

Sadly, she was never going to get better.

Dodge is still paranoid. I suppose it was always there, in his strange abrupt manner, in his inability to look anyone in the face. Not even me.

But the recent upheaval, and the fear of having any contact with the police, had made him even stranger. I wondered more than ever about the experience, presumably during his breakdown, that had set him off. I thought it very unlikely that I would ever find out what happened, though. Certainly not from Dodge himself.

One thing that has been settled is the future of his furniture-making business. He will be continuing without the help of Ben. I think it'll be a relief to both of them. Their differences over the commercial nature of their work were never going to be reconciled, and Dodge is more relaxed operating as a loner.

For Ben the news is more positive. The TOCA Award won by *Riq and Raq* did have consequences. First, it led to his being taken on by an agent, and that agent has now got him a lot of work on major animation projects. My son now has a career path.

I still worry about him. He's currently living with me still, so I can keep an eye on him. But he keeps mentioning new projects his agent's 'in discussion about', and a lot of them would involve his going to the States. I try not to think about it, but I'm pretty sure it's going to happen soon. Someone in his business has to go where the work is.

Ben has, incidentally, now shown me the *Riq and Raq* animation that got him the award. I know I'm his mother but I have to say – it is bloody marvellous! And I get a huge charge from the way Ben's creativity channels Oliver's.

He hasn't mentioned the word 'Pippa' since the TOCA Award night. Am I a real cow to be pleased about that? Probably, yes.

* * *

The news on Jools is not so good. Well, medically she's OK. She had her appointment at St Richard's where it was found that, once the swelling had gone down, the unregulated Hungarian surgeon hadn't made too much of a mess. A bit of tidying-up with some stitches. If that doesn't heal properly, she might need a skin graft. I don't know whose nose she's got now, but it certainly isn't mine.

Once she had had the appointment, however, Jools announced that she was going back to Herne Hill to 'sort things out'. From the description she gave me of her circumstances, they're going to take a lot of 'sorting out'. Her fashion career prospects have crashed and God know how much debt she's got.

Since she's been back in London, nothing. Not a call, not a text, not a WhatsApp. Back like it was before. I worry about her, possibly more than I used to. That period of communication we shared has made me realize how much we could share.

And, as for the cherished image of mother and daughter, in their blue livery polo shirts, working together for SpaceWoman . . . well, forget it.

I had a phone call out of the blue, from Lita Cullingford.

'Did Gerry actually get in touch with you?'

'Yes, he did.'

'What did he want you to do?'

'Clear your sewing stuff out of the garage. Just as I cleared his golf clubs and things.'

'And give them to charity?'

'Yes.'

'Oh, he is a naughty boy,' said Lita. But she said it with great fondness, as if his actions had represented some kind of love token.

I don't know. They say you can never look inside another marriage, but there are some strange folks about.

I doubled my normal rate on the invoices I sent to the Cullingfords. And they paid them meekly. With separate 'compliments' slips. Both thanking me extravagantly for my services. People will never cease to amaze me.

Cedric Waites's funeral, once the police had released his body, was a quiet crematorium affair. Hardly surprising, given how he had cut himself off from human society, that there were few people there. A couple of sober-suited men I didn't recognize, maybe colleagues from the charity he'd worked for. Me, Roy obviously, and Vi Spelling. Tim Goodrich did not attend.

I assumed that Vi might have had some dealings with him over the sale of 14 Seacrest Avenue, but she didn't say anything about it and so Tim's name wasn't mentioned.

The service was short and functional. A vicar who had known nothing of the deceased, murmured some all-purpose platitudes. No one suggested adjourning anywhere for a drink afterwards.

Roy Waites seemed genuinely saddened by the occasion. He felt that his lack of closeness to his father meant his life had been wasted. He told me that Michelle was on remand, awaiting her trial for the murder of Cedric Waites. And he had started divorce proceedings. He also made a point of informing me that he hadn't visited his wife in prison and he had no intention of doing so, whatever kind of sentence she received. He seemed almost gleeful about the situation, the small triumph of a worm finally turning.

I wondered whether life held out something good for him. A pretty student or fellow academic who might restore his faith in womankind. I rather doubted it.

So, there I was, soldiering on. Life back to normal. Whatever that word means.

I had a phone call from Kenneth. 'It's Fleur,' he said. 'She's had a fall. She's in the private patients' bit at St Richard's.'

Of course. She would be.

I was angry. I felt sure she had staged the fall simply to draw attention to herself.

At the same time, I knew there'd come a time when my mother would have falls which weren't staged simply to draw attention to herself.

Guilt reared its ugly head.

When she saw me approaching her bed, Fleur said, 'Oh, I didn't want to trouble you, Ellen darling. I know how busy you are with the cleaning. And I'm actually fine. Kenneth does his best to look after me, now you've stopped bothering.'

Grrr . . .